TAKEN BY THE
HIGHLANDER

ELIZA KNIGHT

ABOUT THE BOOK

1306 - A week before Lady Rose Munro is to wed a neighboring laird, she is abducted on the road by a wicked and dangerously handsome stranger. Highland warrior, Malcolm Montgomery has been ordered by King Robert the Bruce to steal Rose and her son from the suspected traitor she is about to marry—gifting him with an ancient and much sought after dagger as payment. Rose shouldn't trust her captor. Shouldn't feel her body heat at his simple touch, or allow him to press his fervent lips to hers... Malcolm shouldn't be seducing the woman he is sworn to protect. Shouldn't desire her, for she's not meant to be his... Succumbing to passion threatens them both, and falling in love is absolutely not an option.

SECOND EDITION

JULY 2016

Edited by: Andrea Snider

Cover Design: Kimberly Killion @ The Killion Group, Inc.

To my daughters, my princesses, my light.

ACKNOWLEDGMENTS

Many thanks to my amazing Conquered partners, Kris Kennedy, Vonda Sinclair and Jennifer Haymore. And many thanks to my amazing travel/research buddy and editor, Andrea Grant Snider. XOXO

PROLOGUE

Foulis Castle, Scottish Highlands
1297

They were under attack.

Rose, Lady of Munro, grabbed a candlestick—the only thing she could find in her immediate vicinity to use as a weapon. She wrapped her arms around herself and sank to the floor of her solar, grateful she'd had enough energy to at least bar the doors.

Oh, Byron... She chewed on her trembling lip. Rose had tried to grab hold of her husband's hand and begged him to stay with her, but he'd insisted on protecting the castle. He'd told her to hide, then rushed out, his sword drawn, toward the sounds of people screaming and the clanging of weapons.

In her terror, the pains had started in her pregnant belly much too soon. She rubbed a hand over her middle, trying to somehow soothe herself. For the moment, they'd subsided.

Who would attack them?

And why?

Byron had seen to it upon becoming laird of Foulis Castle

that they had excellent fortifications. A stone gate tower was built at the front of the castle walls, with at least half a dozen guards on watch at a time. Byron made sure the gate was always closed, and most often barred. Their walls were thick and impenetrable. If they were being attacked, there should have been fair warning. The guards could see all around the castle. No hidden spots for an enemy to hide. Her husband's retainers kept guard upon the walls and the lands.

So how? Someone from the inside?

Rose drew in a ragged breath, closed her eyes for only a second.

What had she overheard Byron's meddling sister, Myra, railing about? Something about rumors of an impending attack by an ally. But Rose could remember nothing beyond that. And it didn't matter anyway, because they were unquestionably being attacked now.

Rose wasn't certain of how long she'd been on the floor. Her muscles clenched painfully tight, and though the aches in her womb had ceased, the chatter of her teeth had not. It had probably been hours.

And then there was silence.

The sounds of the fighting had stopped. No more screaming. Not even the sound of wood cracking as furniture was overturned. No boots running along the floors or up and down the stairs.

'Twas as if they'd all simply disappeared.

Maybe she was dead, and this was purgatory. Doomed to walk the empty halls of the castle. Being a superstitious sort, Rose pinched herself. It hurt. She wasn't dead.

Well, death may not have yet come, but, she felt in her soul that all was lost, and most importantly, the life of her beloved Byron. Tears of despair welled in her eyes, but after a shuddering half-sob, she forced them not to spill. Not yet.

She had to figure out a way to escape. She'd not yet succumbed to the monsters who'd destroyed her life, her love.

Then she heard it, a faint scratching sound on the wall—Rose jerked back, her hand tightening on the candlestick. The stones beyond her bureau shifted, showing the merest crack of a secret door opening. Rose's mouth fell open, a silent scream on her quivering lips. She'd not known there was a secret door. Surely Byron would have told her if—

"Rose?" came a familiar whisper.

Myra? Could it be? Or simply a figment of her imagination? The opening in the wall looked real enough.

"Hello?" Rose said, tentatively, scrambling awkwardly to her feet. She held the candlestick out in front of her like a weapon. Her eyes burned from the tears she'd yet to shed.

"Rose, 'tis Myra."

Truly? Rose scuffled to the bureau and peered through the crack, seeing Myra's dark hair like a cloud framing her shadowed face.

"Myra!" she whispered frantically. "Ye must help me. They've come. I think they killed Byron. Everyone."

"Who? Wait, help me push this door open, ye must come in here."

Rose shook her head. "They will tear the castle apart looking for survivors. If I come in there, then they will, too."

It would be impossible for them to put the bureau back in place if she pushed it aside to go through the secret entrance. If escape was even possible, and she highly doubted it, then they had to do so unnoticed. The secret passages were the only way—and they had to remain concealed.

Myra licked her lips and spoke with speed. "Can ye get to Byron's library? There's a passage through the hearth."

Rose looked about frantically, expecting the door to her solar to bang open at any moment. It was too quiet. The silence before all hell would break lose. She nodded, fear

3

filling her veins. To leave the sanctuary of her solar... To tread the halls and possibly straight into the arms of the enemy...

But, 'twas the only way.

"I will meet ye there. Go. Quickly." Myra reached her fingers through the door and gripped Rose's, giving her some measure of comfort, however little it was. "I will be there waiting."

Rose nodded again, squeezing Myra's hand with trembling fingers.

Sucking in a ragged, fear-filled breath, Rose said, "I'm going now, Myra."

She tiptoed to the door, placed her hand on the handle but couldn't make herself open it. She closed her eyes, heard Byron's frantic whispers to hide. This was the only way. For several agonizing heartbeats, Rose contemplated. Then she opened the door slowly, and slipped into the darkened hallway. No one struck her down. No one shouted. No one leapt from the darkness. The air smelled stale and she swore she caught the scent of blood.

Rose took a steadying breath, not daring to close her eyes for fear of missing a shadow of an enemy coming toward her. She pressed her hand to her belly, feeling the bairn kick beneath her palm. *Go. Move! You must protect your child, Byron's child.*

Being so close to birth, Rose moved as agilely as she could to the end of the corridor and the circular staircase. One step, two steps, three steps, four... Five steps, six steps, seven, almost there... Rose held her breath as she reached the bottom of the stairs that would lead her up to the next level and Byron's library. How could she do this? If they'd attacked the castle, wouldn't they be looking for his study? The place where all his important papers and treasury were?

Rose stalled, took one step backward, her hand bracing on the stone. What was she thinking?

But, Myra would be there, waiting to take her to safety. She couldn't allow her sister-by-marriage to linger, not when danger was so close at hand. Rose summoned the strength to put first her left foot and then her right onto the stairs, and hoisted herself up once more.

After what felt like forever, she finally made it to the top of the stairs without incident. Silence still reigned with an occasional scream of terror accompanied by a shout of anger. They were picking off her people one by one as they found them. Byron had told their servants to hide, and most of them would do so, but the men more than likely would feel the need to protect, and she couldn't fault them that. They were good people. *Her* good people, and all of them dying.

Pausing at the top of the stairs, Rose listened. When she heard no distinctly human sounds, she tiptoed down the hall, keeping one hand on the wall to help balance her girth. Byron's library door was closed, giving no indication if someone was inside waiting or if the room was completely empty. She pressed her ear to the wood, held her breath and listened. Nothing.

This was it. Now or never.

Her breath hitched and panic threatened to take over, but she willed herself to calm. Willed herself to stay strong for Myra and for her own unborn child's sake.

With trembling fingers she found the handle, twisting until the metal unlatched and then slowly pushed it open. When she saw the library was empty a small whimper of relief escaped her.

Her gaze flew to the library's hidden door within the hearth. Made from plaster to look like stone, it was a perfect disguise within the wall. Soot stained the etchings. There was no fire, and crouched low behind the crack was a shadow.

"Myra?" Rose called softly.

"I'm here." Myra scrambled out of the hidden door in the

hearth, bumping her head on the oak mantel. "Come, we must hurry."

Rose didn't hesitate. *Dear God, let us make it out of here safely.* They were through the secret door, the last inch closing when the main door to the library crashed open. Rose jumped beside Myra, letting out a strangled squeak. Myra reached up, finding Rose's lips in the dark and pinched them, indicating silence as she painstakingly slowly closed the last inch of the secret door.

Rose gripped Myra's hand with deathlike force. *Sweet Lord in Heaven, help us!*

Not waiting to see if those who'd entered happened to notice the wall shift when Myra closed it the remainder of the way, they hurried down the darkened stairs, hands held tightly together. Rose prayed the entire time that the enemy did not follow and for her own stable footing. Already off balance with her huge belly, and not being used to the darkened stairs, she was made all the more unstable. Prayed her body would comply with her urgent need to escape.

They made it to the door leading into the dungeon without even one of the evil villains following.

Myra stopped, her face covered in darkness and gripped Rose's shoulders.

"Listen now, sister. Ye must hide in here. They willna find ye. I promise."

Rose swallowed around the massive lump of fear lodged in her throat. "Where?"

"The dungeon."

Rose shuddered and shook her head.

"Ye must. If they find these tunnels, all is lost. But within the dungeon, they'll not find ye."

She couldn't stay here alone. She couldn't let Myra run off again. They had to get out together. "Where are ye going?"

"I have to find Byron."

Rose gasped. "Nay! Ye canna!" Panic seized Rose, and she was certain she was on the very verge of hysterics. She didn't want Myra to go. Didn't want her to leave her all alone. Knew in her heart... Something was wrong with Byron. He would have come for her. He'd not have left her to her own devices unless—"He's dead..." she whispered.

"Shh... Ye dinna want them to hear us. I willna tarry long. But I must see if he lives."

Rose sobbed quietly and pulled Myra in for a hug. A fool's errand. If he lived, she'd have felt it. Nay, her husband... God rest his soul...

They stood, embracing each other tightly, for as long as Myra would allow, which wasn't nearly long enough, before she pushed the dungeon door open and guided Rose inside.

"Hurry back," Rose said, her voice cracking.

"I will."

Rose slid to the darkened ground of the dungeon, the wetness from the wall seeping through the back of her gown. She crossed her legs in front of her, and clasped her hands in prayer, whispering for strength and perseverance. Finally there was a whisper of footsteps, a swish of skirts and Myra was there again, her torch shining on her face, her expression pinched.

Byron was not with her.

Rose let out a little sob. Though she'd known he was gone from this life, there had been just a tiny spark of hope hidden in her heart.

"We must make haste." Myra's voice came out harshly.

Rose made no comment on it. She knew why. Her husband was gone, and Myra had had to witness his body, spirit departed. Poor lass.

The father of her child. Murdered by an enemy, someone who'd supposedly been close to them. When Rose didn't move, Myra pulled her to her feet and led her back into the

7

darkened corridor, tugging her along as they made their way farther down the stairs.

"We will have to crawl through here. Think ye can manage?" Myra asked.

"Aye," Rose said, her voice coming out hard and edged with ice. There was no time to mourn. No time to feel sad for the life of a handsome man who had been taken too soon.

They crawled through the last tunnel, the weight of the castle above them. The stones were slick and bits of debris littering the floor jabbed into her palms.

Ye can do this. Rose repeated the words in her mind a thousand times, and with each recitation, she felt a little stronger.

When they neared the end of the tunnel, a bright light slipped through a crack of stone, beckoning them forward. A breeze whistled through the fissure sending wintry chills up and down her limbs. 'Twas cold outside... Traveling would not be easy.

"We're almost there," Myra called to Rose who crawled behind her.

Rose let out a little grunt.

"Keep that bairn inside ye."

"He's to stay put," Rose panted from the exertion of crawling.

"Let us pray 'tis a boy."

Aye, she did pray it was so, for her son would inherit Foulis and be Chief of Clan Munro, and perhaps she could find someone to champion her bairn, take up arms and reclaim what had been stolen from them. They at last reached the end where there was room to stand. Myra helped Rose up, her legs wobbly.

"When we leave this cave, we will have to keep close to the walls, and ye'll need to stay hidden while I fetch us a horse," Myra said.

"Nay!" Rose shook her head vehemently. They would only

end up getting killed. "The attackers are sure to be out there."

"Aye. But what choice do we have? We canna stay here and wait for them to find us."

In the sliver of light coming from the hidden entrance, Rose studied Myra's determination. Though she was heavy with child, Rose wasn't going to let Myra walk into a trap. She could still protect her, or at least try.

"We shall walk into the village and get a horse from there," Rose offered.

Myra shook her head. "Most likely they've burned the village, or at the very least are looting it. I'll not have us stuck there." Myra pressed a steady hand to Rose's belly, feeling the child kick within. "Or be killed. We will see my brother's heir to safety. Ye and I together."

Rose let out a shuddering breath. If there was anyone who could get them to safety, it was Myra. "I trust ye." Rose nodded, her eyes wide. "I do."

"All right, then, ye stay here. If I'm not back within a quarter hour, run."

I will never be weak again.

❧ I ❧

Foulis Castle
Spring, 1306

"**A** good morning to ye, Giddy." Lady Rose Munro stared at the beautiful chestnut mare eating quite happily in the stable. The lazy mount was happier munching on hay in her stall than roaming the moors to eat fresh grass. Exactly the opposite of her sire, Coney, the warhorse who'd brought Myra and Rose to the safety of Dunrobin Castle all those years before, when Foulis was attacked. That fated day that changed the course of her life.

Without Coney, they'd have been lost to the enemy for certain.

To honor him, she'd taken Giddy with her and spoiled her rotten.

Giddy's penchant for laziness only lasted as long as the walk to freedom and then the mare could soar over the moors faster than some chargers.

"Shall I get her ready for ye, my lady?" the stable master asked.

Rose smiled. "I dinna want to take ye away from your duties. I know plenty of the mares have already begun foaling this week."

"Aye, happy I am that spring has come." He rocked proudly on his heels.

"As am I." While pretty white landscapes with crystals of ice were a beautiful sight to behold, the bitter cold had kept Rose and her son, Byron II, cooped up inside the long winter months. Now that spring had arrived, Byron was off running around with a few of the clan lads his age, along with his three slobbery hounds, and she was ready for a brisk ride upon the open moors.

Rose opened the stall, receiving a cranky snort from Giddy, which she ignored. She brushed her hand over her horse's withers, whispering sweet nonsense as she readied Giddy. Already, the surge of excitement that riding brought pumped through her veins.

"Out ye go, pretty," Rose cooed, earning a little nuzzle from Giddy.

Exiting the stables, she was greeted by six of her guard.

Peter, the head of her personal guard, stared down at her with a raised brow. "Now, my lady, did ye think we'd let ye go out unescorted?" he teased.

Rose rolled her eyes. "I'd not dream of it." Nine years had passed since their castle was seized by Ross and his men. And while they'd gotten back the castle, and her son was safe, the whole of Scotland was still blanketed in unrest. Battles and ambushes from the English were not uncommon. Though, she hoped this far north, the brunt of it would stay clear of them. Still, she was grateful for the warriors who guarded her son, too young yet at only nine years of age, to lead his people alone.

"Will ye be needing a hand?" Peter offered.

Rose shook her head, took hold of the saddle and hoisted

herself in place. She settled astride, hating the more proper way to ride sidesaddle. If she wanted to feel the air in her hair and smell the blooms of heather through the fields, then she was going to bloody well enjoy it!

Rose urged Giddy through the gate, her guards in tow. Her mount pranced and whinnied, gnashing at the bit, but as soon as they'd crossed over the bridge covering the moat, and the gentle breeze ruffled her mane, the horse leapt into gallop. Rose's smile broadened and she sucked in the crisp spring air. Though the sun shone down on her, there was still a bite to the air that sent a shiver of a thrill over her skin.

Soon, she could have a husband at her side for these rides. Myra, her sister-by-marriage, and her husband, Laird Daniel Murray, had helped her to arrange a new husband and ally that could be trusted to help raise her son into being the laird he ought to be. Though she'd tried her best over the past nine years, even going so far as to send young Byron to stay with Daniel and Myra for months at a time, it wasn't the same as having a laird he could look up to.

Cathal MacKenzie.

He was an older man, fifteen years her senior, but he was a laird with experience, and his lands bordered hers on two sides. Munro lands accessed the Firth leading out to the North Sea, and with only a boy as their chief, they were vulnerable to attack, though they'd been lucky the last nine years to avoid it. She was grateful to the men Myra's husband kept stationed on Munro lands to guard the North Sea, since any enemy could have access to the Highlands through her lands. But that couldn't last. Marriage to Cathal was not only a strategic move, bringing peace to her people, but also for added protection. She wasn't in love with him, didn't even know him well enough to say whether or not she liked him. But she had agreed to marry him for the sake of her clan.

The previous year, William Wallace was arrested and

executed by the English. If their great guardian could come to such a fate, what would happen to the rest of them? Daniel had been close to Wallace, and had mourned the loss greatly. But he'd also been warned of impending sieges from the English, a renewed attempt on the part of their vicious king to control the Highlands. Truth was, the Munros needed the support of the MacKenzies against the English, even if it did mean the likelihood that she'd leave her life as a Munro behind and so would her son, at least until he could take possession of his position by birthright.

Part of the contract that Daniel had helped to formulate stipulated that upon his eighteenth birthday, her son Byron, would take his place as Chief Munro, but until that time, her husband would be his guardian, a prospect that was a little daunting.

Rose closed her eyes for a brief second, sucking in the chill spring air and letting go, just for this moment, the stress of her impending marriage. She'd loved her first husband fiercely, and she knew that such emotions could not be recreated. This marriage was simply a convenience and to ally their clans.

A thunking sound in the road ahead, and a shout of warning from her men, had Rose's eyes popping open and she twisted in the saddle to see what her men were worried about. A breeze blew against the leaves of the trees, rustling them ominously. The road appeared clear. At least at first, she saw nothing, then she spotted it—an arrow in the center of the road with a red strip of fabric tied to its shaft and blowing with the wind.

"What is happening?" she asked. She shouldn't have closed her eyes. That must have been when the arrow was shot.

"Stay back, my lady," Peter shouted. He rushed to stand

before her and the other five guards followed suit, forming a circle in front of her.

They reined in their horses, their swords drawn and held out, waiting for whoever it was that had shot the warning arrow.

They didn't have to wait long.

From the trees, perhaps twenty yards away, the muzzle of a massive black warhorse appeared, covered in shining armor that reached to his ears, which were held back in warning. A reflection on his master. Massive paws clomped slowly on the ground, like a demon sent from the underworld to take her. His master was equally impressive. Tall and thick, he sat the horse with expert ease, but the sheer size of him alone sent her heart into palpitations. Over a linen shirt, he wore a plaid she didn't recognize, colors as green as the grass and blue as the sky. A thick iron brooch in the shape of a dragon. Leather boots covered his muscled calves to his knees, and a gleaming silver sword was held in one hand. Hair she thought at first to be brown, gleamed red in the light of the sun. His face was painted in lines and swirls of blue.

Rose shook in the saddle, causing her own horse to shift restlessly beneath her. She dragged in a ragged breath, and bit her lip to keep her teeth from chattering.

"Dear God, save us," one of her men muttered under his breath.

The warrior stared them down with an intensity that could have melted iron. His eyes met hers, locking her in, making her limbs go weak and numb. They were the color of storm clouds, and she swore if he looked up at the sky, he could command lightning to strike.

"Do not engage him," she whispered. "Negotiate."

"I dinna think the man has negotiating in mind," Peter said.

Rose's belly twisted into knots. She didn't want her men

to lose their lives, not in protecting her. They were low on men as it was. However, Peter was right. One look at the fierce warrior and she could glean that he never negotiated.

"Then we should turn and run now. We might be able to beat them back to the castle," she urged, trying to save her men.

"Aye, my lady, I think ye're right." Peter nodded to the men and as one they whipped their horses around and kicked their flanks, Rose doing the same, until their horses fairly flew across the moors.

From behind she could hear the pounding of the warhorse accompanied by even more. How many had he brought with him? They made not a sound as they advanced, and with every passing second, Rose grew more fearful. The castle was still a good distance away. They'd not make it through the gates to safety in time.

Was this to be her fate? Having survived a brutal attack at the hands of her enemies nine years before, only to die by a demon warrior in the middle of the moors, buried forever in the bogs?

"Hurry!" Peter bellowed.

But his urging was all for naught. Behind her, she heard the painful cry of one of her men, and turning slightly in her saddle, she watched as the man was hit on top of the head with the hilt of a sword by one of the painted demons accompanying the warrior.

He didn't stop.

He kept coming.

His eyes on her and her alone.

A shiver raced over her spine. Pure, blinding terror. A sound, guttural and feral, fell from her lips.

He was going to kill her. Possibly roast her and eat her, picking her flesh from his teeth with her bones.

"God's bones... I am lost," she said, teeth chattering.

"Rose!" Peter shouted. "Come on!"

She turned back to the front, intent on their course, leaning over the withers of her horse. "Go, Giddy! Please!" she begged.

If the mellow horse would only push herself as her father Coney had all those years before. Giddy seemed to sense her urgency, picking up speed, but with each step forward, she heard the thunder of the warrior growing closer. And then another of her men was picked off by the demon's minions.

"We'll not make it. We have to engage," Peter ground out. He reined in his horse and the men followed, turning around to combat the men who'd ambushed them. "Go, Rose! We'll try to hold them off."

For a brief second she thought to argue, but there was no way she could save her men, not with the tiny blade strapped at her waist. The best thing she could do was get out of their way and warn her people to get within the walls, safeguarding them against what could very well be an attack on the castle itself.

The clashing of swords sounded behind her as the men fought the warriors. Shouts of pain and bellows of anger pounded through her head.

"No, no, no," Rose muttered, tears stinging her eyes.

How naïve she'd been to think that after nine years she'd be safe. Who were these men that had attacked? Not Mackenzies. And it would seem even a contract between the two of them hadn't kept her safe, though she'd yet to wed Cathal.

She didn't recognize any of the men who'd ambushed them, nor the colors of their plaid. They were strangers. But they'd come with a purpose. They didn't look rough enough to be outlaws, but what did Rose truly know about the ways of outlaws? They could be anyone. From anywhere.

The pounding grew closer to her and a peek over her

shoulder showed that while her men fought for their lives behind her, that the leader of the warriors had not stopped. He was only a few feet away!

Rose screamed as he closed the distance. He reached for her, wrapping strong, gloved hands around her waist and yanking her from her saddle. The warrior tossed her over his lap, Giddy continuing on the path toward the castle with Rose no longer seated on her back. His thighs were hard against her belly, her legs dangling on one side of the horse, her head and arms on the other. The man didn't slow down, but made a wide circle back toward the fray.

"Don't touch me! Put me down!" Rose cried, tears of fear turning to tears of anger. She pounded at his calf with her fists and bucked and kicked, but he smacked her rear and pressed hard on her spine.

A flash of metal before her face and he held a ruby-hilted dagger to her throat. "Be still, or I won't hesitate to bind ye." His voice was deep and rough and sent her fear into overdrive.

"Ye'll have to kill me first!" Rose wasn't going to give in. She bucked harder at the injustice of her position.

"Ye may wish for death, my lady, but 'tis a gift I'll not be giving ye." And with that, the dagger was gone, and he was still riding away with her.

2

The lass was warm and her curves were soft.

Malcolm Montgomery gritted his teeth against the flailing woman, her plump breasts pressed into his thigh, and the curve of her bottom still burned to the flat of his palm. The ruby dagger in his grip was a lovely gift, an ancient relic that Robert the Bruce, newly crowned King of Scotland cherished and had given to Malcolm for his service to the Scottish Royal Council. The King Richard Dagger.

Except it wasn't truly a gift for Malcolm. It was only the beginning of payment for the task at hand.

Malcolm had been charged with stealing the bride of Cathal Mackenzie—currently under suspicion of treason to the Scottish people and the Bruce himself.

Mackenzie, bastard that he was, had somehow finagled his way into the good graces of the Murrays, cousins to William Wallace, and garnered himself a prime bride—and full control of the Moray and Cromarty Firths that led straight into the North Sea.

A letter intercepted by one of the Bruce's spies confirmed that Mackenzie planned to take over those ports and allow the English Navy to moor their ships and march their troops straight into the heart of the Highlands.

But without a bride to wed, the man would have a much harder time gaining control. He'd have to take it forcibly, which would be hard to do, considering Malcolm had already sent another flank of his own men ahead to the castle.

"Put me down!" the wench wrestled against his lap.

His groin tightened at her movements and how her warm breasts rubbed over his thigh. Damnation, now was not the time to be thinking lusty thoughts, and if she wasn't careful, her ribs were about to find out just what was going through his head. Thank the saints for his second-in-command and childhood mate, Kavan. Malcolm could concentrate on the feisty wench, while Kavan kept the men in line and the scouts reporting.

"I'll not be putting ye down, lass. Calm yourself, else ye end up hurt."

"Please, I beg ye."

"Ye can beg until ye're out of breath, but I canna let ye go, Lady Munro."

"Who are ye?" she asked, turning to stare up at him, her creamy cheeks tinged rosy and her lips pulled back in a snarl. Locks of burnished gold hung in wild curls around her face. Green eyes filled with tears and burned with fury. "What kind of monster are ye?"

"I'm not a monster, even if ye think it."

She stilled in her writhing, eyes locking on his and a hatred so potent in their depths, he could nearly feel the singe. "Only a monster would steal an unsuspecting woman from her first spring ride."

Malcolm shrugged. "I doubt that."

"Tell me your name," she said. "Ye already know mine."

"My name is not important," he said, growing irritated

with the back and forth. Didn't she know that when taken prisoner, a lass should keep her pretty mouth shut?

"Then I shall call ye Satan, for the verra devil ye are."

That made Malcolm laugh. He'd been called many things in his life, devil even one of them, but none had gone so far as to call him Satan. "Perhaps Lucifer would be better to your taste, my lady?" he asked.

Hearing his name, Malcolm's horse pricked his ears and let out a little snort.

The skirmish was well behind them. His men were under strict orders not to take any of her foolish guards' lives, simply to render them unconscious, or let them go. They'd put up a good fight to keep their lady safe, but none of them had dealt with the Dragon, fiercest guard on the Bruce's council.

The lass planted her cheek against his thigh and for a minute he feared she'd bite him. Above the sound of his horse's hoof beats, he could swear he heard her praying.

He should put her at ease, or at least attempt to do so. Likely she was frightened to death, and if he were willing to admit it, having grown up with a sister himself, he'd hate it if someone were to steal her away.

Malcolm awkwardly patted her back, but the move only sent the woman into another tailspin of bucking.

"Dinna touch me!" she shouted.

Lord help him, this was going to be a very long ride.

"My lady, let me assure ye, I dinna intend to do ye harm. I am simply a messenger."

"Messengers dinna kill people and abduct ladies!" Her voice was filled with venom and once more she'd twisted to stare at him, catching him off guard with just how lovely she was when angry.

"This is true, I am a little more than a messenger." He left out the plain truth of not having killed her men either. Perhaps fear of such would keep her quiet.

"What do ye intend to do with me, if ye didna have killing in mind? Ye want to rape me? I'll scratch your eyes out!" Without a second's pause she bit him, planting her solid teeth into the bare flesh above his knee and sinking deep.

Malcolm roared, his legs flexing. Used to his master's movements when in battle, Lucifer was immediately on guard for who had attacked, and when his ears piqued toward the lass in Malcolm's lap, he bucked. Lady Munro wobbled on his legs, and he kept his grip on her until Lucifer reared his head back, smacking into Malcolm's forehead and then bucking mightily.

"*Arrêt!*" Malcolm shouted for his horse to stop in French, the language he'd used to train his mount so that he'd not become confused on the battlefield with a thousand other commands in Gaelic or English.

Lucifer ceased his wild behavior but it was too late.

The two of them toppled off the horse.

Malcolm managed to land somewhat gracefully with one foot and one knee on the ground, and the lass just a few feet away from him, wasted no time in scrambling to her feet and running.

Malcolm rolled his eyes and commanded his horse to stay put. "*Rester!*"

The damned animal contentedly munched on grass as if nothing had happened. He'd have to send the beast back into the ring for this. Never had his mount betrayed him as he'd just done. Malcolm faced the scrambling lass. She ran, but continued to falter in her steps as she turned to see if he was coming. Had no one ever taught her to simply run from an enemy and not look back?

He took off at a steady clip toward her, each of his long strides easily taking up two or three of her own, and then he had her, wrapping his hands around her tiny waist and hauling her back against his body.

"Use your teeth on me again and I'll bend ye over my knee to smack your arse until it is red as a rose."

She gasped, and slammed her head back, missing his chin by an inch. She jabbed her elbow against his ribs, and he grunted at the pain of it, then circled both arms around her, pinning her arms at her side. She pushed her hips back, bucking, the soft curve of her arse deliciously melding with his groin. Malcolm groaned. The lady heaved her breaths, each rise and fall causing the undersides of her breasts to brush his arms.

He gritted his teeth.

Since meeting the lass less than an hour before, he'd become more intimately acquainted with her breasts and rear than he had with a lass in awhile.

Why had he waited so long? The torment of his decision to focus on his duties to king and country instead of more pleasurable pursuits was coming back to haunt him.

And just like that, Malcolm was certain he had a way of calming her—well, perhaps not calming her, but getting her to stop her movements. He leaned low, his lips brushing the shell of her ear.

"Cease this at once," he hissed. "Else I make good on the promises ye keep making."

"Promises?" she gasped.

"Aye. Ye are merciless in your desire for me. The way ye move against me. Ye taunt me, lass, and I am but a man." He clenched his teeth to keep from laughing.

The lass stiffened instantly letting loose a shocking gasp. "I have made no such promises! I seek only to get away from ye."

"Ye will not succeed."

She blew out a long ragged breath, perhaps resigned to that truth. "Why have ye taken me? Where are we going?"

"Do ye promise to cooperate if I tell ye?" He kept his arms wrapped around her, his lips on her ear.

"I canna make such a promise. Is it not the will of a prisoner to escape?"

"'Haps when ye hear ye'll think differently."

"I doubt it."

Malcolm shrugged, picked her up and tossed her over his shoulder. "When ye do feel inclined to cooperate, I'll fill ye in."

"Put me down!" She beat her fists against his back.

Malcolm's patience was growing thin. He slapped her bottom and called out, "Behave, wench, else I make good and gag ye and tie up your wrists."

She stopped moving. And he thought he'd gotten lucky, except when he planted her on his horse he could see the track of tears staining her cheeks.

He blew out a frustrated breath and climbed behind her, feeling marginally guilty for being such a lout. "I am taking ye to Kildrummy Castle."

"Kildrummy?"

"Aye." Why the hell did he feel the need to tell her that? Maybe because those tears had been real and he didn't fancy himself an abductor. Aye, that was essentially what he was, but in truth, he was a warrior and a damned good one. He honored the weak and protected them. That didn't mean he couldn't exact punishment when it was warranted. But the lady had done nothing to warrant a punishment. She'd simply planned to marry a traitor. And god help her if she knew that.

"Is that not the current seat of the Bruce?"

"Aye." He blew out a breath having somewhat of an idea where she was going with this. She'd be disappointed when she found out the Bruce had been part of the plan.

"I am going to tell him of your treatment of me!"

"Your threat will do little good."

She was silent a moment, and he hoped to get in a few miles of peace before she spoke again.

A hope that was quickly dashed.

"Please, ye canna take me. Not without my son! He will be panicked when I do not return and he's already lost enough in his short life."

"Ye need not fear for your son, my lady. I have arranged for him to meet ye at Kildrummy." At least one good deed he'd done.

"Meet me..." Her voice trailed off.

"Ye have planned this."

"Aye."

"But why?"

"I shall let the Bruce explain that to ye."

"I have done nothing wrong," she said, her voice quivering.

"Are ye certain?" If she did in fact know about Mackenzie's plan to allow the English into the Highlands, then she would be an accomplice. A traitor.

And that would open up a whole new world of information. For if the lass was a traitor, that meant the Murrays were traitors, didn't it? But nay, they could not be. Why would they allow the very murderers of their kinsman William Wallace into their homelands to murder them too? They wouldn't.

"I have done nothing wrong. I am ever loyal to the Bruce and his cause. My husband was loyal to our country. He was killed by a traitor and ye insult me with your words."

"Apologies, my lady. I meant no offense." How absurd that he should find himself apologizing to the woman he'd abducted in the name of his newly appointed king. Malcolm rolled his eyes.

"Ye have offended me greatly. Why could ye not simply

come to me with a message to speak with the king? This is a farce! I dinna believe ye! If harm comes to my son, I will carve out your heart with the first stick or stone I find!" The vehemence in her voice was paralyzing. The woman had grit, he had to give her that.

And hell, he respected her for it, too.

"No harm will come to your son. Ye have my word."

"Your word means nothing. Ye're a common outlaw, a criminal, an abuser of woman."

Malcolm sighed with resignation.

"I assure ye, my lady, I am none of those things."

"Prove it. Take me back to my castle."

℈ 3 ℈

Rose knew that when you bargained with the devil, sometimes you got burned.

And she fully expected Lucifer to tie her up and gag her for all the trouble she'd given him in abducting her. Her only saving grace was that if he were to take her to Kildrummy Castle she could speak with the king about the injustice.

Though, the king scared her half to death. Why was he summoning her? And her son?

Oh, saints, but young Byron had to be filled with panic and fear. The poor lad was only nine summers!

She craned her neck to look at her captor. Stared up into his swirling stormy eyes. Nervous tingles shot up and down her limbs. The way he stared at her, so intense, and yet, she couldn't read a single thought that crossed his mind. What could he be thinking? Did she really want to know?

"Ye dare to challenge me?" he asked, his voice low and rasping.

How to answer? Rose chewed her lip, afraid to say anything and yet terrified not to say anything at all. Silence would not help her cause. She took in a few shuddering, cleansing breaths, hoping to ease the waiver she was certain would be in her voice.

"Take me back to Foulis." She met his gaze, unwavering. "Take me back to my son."

The warrior shook his head. "As I told ye. Your son is not there."

The man was insistent on that point. She didn't want to believe him, but his tone was so confident. "How can ye be certain? We have guards upon the wall, what's to say that your men were successful in breaching our defenses?"

He grinned, cocky arrogance rippling through his body. She wanted to slap him.

"Trust me," he said. "Your walls were breached."

Rose squeezed her eyes shut a moment. "I dinna understand. Why take us? Why fight to take us when a simple missive would do?"

"That is where ye're wrong, my lady. A simple missive would not have provided the message we sought."

In frustration, she fisted her hands and slammed them on her thighs. "Message to who? To me? Am I to believe that after a lifetime of loyalty to the king that I am not worthy of respect?"

The warrior issued a command to his warhorse in French, of all languages, and obediently, the animal picked up his pace until they were galloping.

"The message was not to ye," he finally answered, staring straight ahead, no longer meeting her eyes.

That stunned her into silence. She turned away from him to stare at the horse's mane, trying to wrap her head around his words. Who could the king, by way of this warrior, intend to send a message to?

"My people are nothing but loyal," she whispered.

"'Haps. But the message was not to them either."

Rose gripped the front of the saddle, willing herself not to start screaming like a banshee. Did the jackanapes have any idea how infuriating he was? "Then who? I beg ye to tell me."

"Ye're an inquisitive wench."

Gahhhh! Rose gritted her teeth. "And ye're a close-mouthed boor. I do not even know your name with which to deride ye."

The man grunted, perhaps even a hint of a chuckle. "Ye can call me Montgomery."

"Montgomery?" Obviously a family or clan name. The name was familiar to her. She thought back through the years to see where she'd heard the name before, and then she knew. After she'd escaped the attack at her castle that killed her husband, with Myra's help, she'd made it to Dunrobin Castle, seat of Chief Sutherland. His sister, Lorna, was married to Laird Jamie Montgomery.

"Aye, that it is."

Rose worried her lower lip, not wanting to sound too eager when she spoke to him, nor too enthusiastic, though since he'd not picked up on her frustration, he'd likely not pick up on any other emotions either. "Are ye any relation to Laird Montgomery?"

The man stiffened behind her. She could imagine how his brows must be furrowed. "What do ye know of him?"

Presenting her knowledge and connection slowly was the best course of action. "He is married to Lorna Sutherland."

"He is." Oh, if his brows could talk, she had no doubt one just winged another inch.

She seemed to have finally caught his attention.

"I am allied to the Sutherlands," she said smugly.

"And ye're hoping that alliance extends to me?"

Oh, dear heavens, this didn't sound promising...

"I'll give ye credit for thinking such, lass, and ye are right, but the thing is, I've been tasked by my king in retrieving ye, and I obey the orders of my sovereign. Now cease your questions." His tone was firm, and held no room for argument, though that was exactly what she wanted to do.

She wanted to rail against the injustice of it. At least she'd gotten in one good bite, though it was no comparison to the emotional trauma he was causing her.

The sudden intrusion of pounding hoof beats behind them had her panicking, and hopeful at the same time. Had her men come after her? Montgomery didn't seem to care at all, and she soon knew why. His men pulled up beside them, a few with bloodied noses or black eyes. Her men had put up a fight... Yet, if these men had returned, her men had not won.

She felt sick to her stomach. Saints, but she hoped Peter and the rest of them had made it out alive. Back to the safety of the castle—but no! The castle was not safe!

Rose glanced at the men out of the corners of her eyes, wanting desperately to ask but too afraid that one more question would only gain her a rag in the mouth.

As they crossed over the moors and up into the ridges of the forest, all Rose could do was pray that her son was indeed safe, and that if what Montgomery said was true, she'd be reunited with him very shortly. She prayed for her men. For her people. Worked herself up until she was sick, her stomach burning with the worry she felt.

They rode for most of the day, and by the time they finally stopped for the night, Rose's body was screaming for relief. Her bladder felt ready to burst and her buttocks were sore, her feet numb. She squeezed her eyes, wishing that when she opened them, these men, this camp, the horror of the day, would all disappear.

It did not.

She could smell the sweat of the men, the leather of the horses, the untouched scents of nature oblivious to her peril.

Montgomery climbed down from behind and held up his

hands. She shook her head, not wanting his help at all. If it weren't for him, she wouldn't even be in this mess. But he didn't listen. He grabbed her around the waist and hauled her off the horse; the touch of his palms against her middle was suddenly and unwelcomingly warm and inviting.

Rose shoved his hands away when her feet were firmly planted on the ground.

They had the protection of the trees at their backs and a loch at their front. The sky overhead was beginning to darken, and a few caws and hoots from night birds of prey shifted with the wind. The men had already dismounted and were setting up camp. Rose looked around, trying to find the right spot for a bit of privacy when Montgomery gripped her elbow.

"This way," he said.

"I can walk by myself." She tried to yank free of his touch.

He held tighter. "I can see that, but I'll escort ye all the same."

Rose pressed her lips together, frowning and yanked with all her might until her elbow was free, only to feel his hand press against the small of her back. A rumble of a scream started in her belly, but she squashed it.

She was not free.

Once again she was struck with how this man had touched her in more places than any other since her husband. Not only was the idea of it disconcerting, but so was the way her body seemed to warm with each touch.

"This bush will do," he said.

"Pardon me?" she asked, raising a brow. The warrior was incredibly bossy, to believe he could tell her just where to relieve herself. Rose stopped short and crossed her arms over her chest, a petulant frown on her face, not unlike the ones she'd seen on her son many a time.

"Go behind it. Relieve yourself. I'll be right here. Waiting."

The bush was two feet away from him. Hardly private. She pointed to another about a dozen paces away. "That one will do better for me."

Montgomery glowered at her for the span of several heart beats, to the point where she nearly gave up, but she must have outlasted his will by a mere second or two.

He let out a long, exasperated sigh, then grumbled, "As ye wish."

Rose was astonished to have won something, even if it was as simple as a bush in which to hide behind. She went forth to do her business, wondering how easy it would be to escape. Doing so though was out of the question. If Montgomery truly did have her son, then her trying to run away would only create a problem. And she had to get her son back. Chancing his safety was not an option.

She emerged from behind the bush to find Montgomery leaning his bulky body against a tree and fiddling with his ruby dagger.

"I would like to wash by the water."

He glanced up at her, piercing her with those gray eyes, making her feel as though he could see into her very soul. He nodded. They walked toward the loch, again his hand pressing against her back and with each step the tension inside her mounted, coiling in her belly, around her ribs and her throat. It was a mixture of nerves and sensuality entwined in a big pulsing ball. She felt ready to explode.

She knelt on shaky knees to the ground and cupped water in her hands, hoping the splash of cool liquid on her over-heated face would help to calm her. But it didn't, so she splashed again, rubbing her hands in the water and then over her neck. The chilled water sluiced over her skin sneaking into her gown and finding its way over her spine. Even with the water cooling her skin, she felt hot.

Montgomery stooped beside her. His long fingers dipped into the water and splashing it over his face and neck, a mirror image. She spied him from the corner of her eyes, her heart pounding and her mind racing with unanswered questions.

Well, enough was enough, she was no timid lass. She'd learned to be strong over the last near decade. "Where is my son?" she demanded.

He glanced over toward her, water dripping from his face and pooling in large drips from his chin. She followed the path of the water, her eyes stopping momentarily to gaze at his mouth before realizing what she was doing and jerking her eyes upward.

Montgomery grinned. "He is with my men."

If he was willing to answer her without reminding her of her place, then perhaps she could dig a little deeper with her demands. "I want to see him. I need to know he is safe."

"Ye have my word, that is enough."

Frustration streaked an angry red path through her veins. "Your word means nothing." Rose stood, hands fisted at her sides.

Montgomery, too, stood, anger slicing over his features. "My word means everything."

She didn't back down. Even with the warrior standing nearly a foot taller than her, easily twice as broad, she wasn't going to show her fear. "It means *nothing* to me."

He grimaced, his teeth flashing in the moonlight "Then ye're a fool."

"I am no more a fool than the man who abducts a woman and thinks she should trust him," she retorted.

He cocked his head, eyes narrowing as he studied her. "Ye have a point."

That startled her. He agreed? She faltered, words getting caught in her throat. Not the reaction she was expecting. At all. "I want to see my son. Now."

He swiped a frustrated hand over his face. "I cannot comply with your wish."

"Where is he? How far is he? Take me to him."

Montgomery shook his head. "'Tis impossible. For safety, we must keep the two of ye separate until we reach Kildrummy."

"Safety from whom?" Her voice was growing in octaves. She'd be raving mad in a moment; she could feel the anger burning through her chest.

"There is much ye dinna understand. And I dinna expect ye to understand everything, being a woman."

What? Her mouth fell agape. Thoroughly insulted, even if she shouldn't have expected anything less from the man.

Nevertheless, that was the last straw. Rose's patience had a limit and her temper broke free from its bonds. She flew at him, hands balled and raised. She wailed at him, but he caught each of her fisted palms, wrapping his arms around her, pinning her elbows to her ribs, and when she tried to kick him, he pinned her legs between his thick, muscled thighs.

"Stop this!" he hissed.

Rose shook and heaved, glaring up at him. She spewed venom, calling him names she'd heard her men shout while practicing in the fields. One of which, she knew was particularly vulgar. And then, suddenly, his lips were crushed against hers. Silencing her with warm, firm, velvet. She was not prepared for the strength of her own body's reaction. The intensity in which she pressed her lips back.

Montgomery's hands slid to her shoulders, her arms no longer pinned. He cupped her cheeks, dipped his head to the side and kissed her deeper.

What was happening? Why was he kissing her?

Frissons of unexpected pleasure fired along her nerves. Her entire body trembled with both fear and excitement.

Why did she like his kiss? This was wrong. Incredibly so.

He was her captor. Had stolen her and her son away from the safety of their castle, and she was letting him kiss her?

Nay. She could not.

Rose jerked back and slapped him hard on the cheek, her teeth bared. "Dinna do that ever again, ye jackanapes."

Montgomery touched the place she'd struck him and cleared his throat. "'Twas the only way to get ye to shut up."

With that, the blasted warrior lifted her up and tossed her over his shoulder. He marched back to the quiet, smoky camp with her too stunned to speak, his shoulder digging painfully into her belly.

Montgomery lifted the flap of a tent, ducked inside and fairly tossed her into a pile of thick woolen blankets. He knelt in front of her, yanking a strip of rope from somewhere and wrapped it around her wrists—although not very tight. The entire time, the muscle in his jaw worked and his glower was hot enough to melt ice, or perhaps it was cold enough to freeze rain. Rose couldn't decide.

All she knew was that she should be frightened by this man, and she wasn't. Perhaps that was the most frightening thing of all.

"Another word, and this goes in your mouth." He held up a square of linen, hardly the raggedly old cloth she thought he'd use.

Rose nodded.

"Where did ye even learn to speak that way?" He shook his head. "If my sister had ever called me a—" He stopped abruptly. "Well, I'll not repeat it in the presence of a female, but if she'd ever even uttered that word, my Da would have taken her over his knee. 'Haps I ought to do that to ye, just to teach ye a lesson."

Rose made a point of clamping her lips closed and glaring at him.

Montgomery grunted. "I see ye've learned your lesson. I'll go and fetch ye some supper."

And then he was gone, and Rose let out a deep, ragged breath, collapsing onto the woolen blankets, tears spilling from her eyes.

4

Sleep deserted Malcolm.

Every time he'd closed his eyes he only ended up seeing the feisty, enticing wench trying to fight him, felt her warm lips pressed to his. Sensed the fight leave her only to be replaced with an urgent passion.

What in bloody hell was wrong with him?

Aye, he'd kissed her to shut her up, but also because he couldn't imagine going through another day without kissing her. Because from the moment he'd seen her, he'd been drawn to her by some invisible force.

Bah! It was all rubbish.

Not enough sleep. The rush of battle whirling in his blood.

Most warriors needed a woman to slake the pent up excitement. That was all it was. She was the first woman he'd seen, and her curves had been pressed to his body for hours.

But the thing was, Malcolm wasn't like all the other warriors. He wasn't a man who immediately needed to sink his cock inside a woman simply because he'd sunk his sword into one man or a dozen.

Malcolm wasn't the sort of man to simply take a woman for the pleasure of it. In fact, he was exactly the opposite. His own pledge to ward off the sins of the flesh in order to concentrate more fully on his duties to the king were now in serious peril.

All because of one unruly woman.

She wasn't even the type of lass he normally was attracted to.

Rose was not a fresh young maiden in need of teaching.

Rose was a woman who had knowledge of a man. Widowed and a mother, she had more experience than any other woman he'd ever kissed. And though their brush of lips had been short, and hasty, it was still not the fumbling mouth of someone with inexperience.

Och! What in bloody hell was he thinking?

Malcolm had only lain through the night with his thoughts for mayhap an hour no more before going and taking a post on watch. Not wanting his men to know what was really wrong, he only remarked that he was still feeling the rush of battle, which wasn't actually a lie. Morning greeted him, but he did not reply with luster as he normally did.

"Montgomery." The sound of his name on her lips was enough to make him start against the tree he'd been leaning against. He opened his eyes and stared at her, a gorgeous, unruly vision before him.

Her blonde curls were in even more disarray than they'd been the day before. Her green gown was rumpled and her arms were stretched out before her, still tied at the wrists.

He was a bloody monster.

When he'd brought her something to eat, she'd been worked up into such a rage, she started throwing the food at his head, and he'd been convinced the only way to get her to stop was to tie her wrists once more.

Malcolm yanked the jeweled dagger from the strap at his waist and skimmed it between her wrists. With a quick flick, the rope was cut and her hands free. She pulled them to herself, rubbing at the soreness.

"Thank ye," she said, eyes toward the ground.

She looked rejected and he hated that. He didn't want to see her so cowed by anything, anyone. Her spirit was beautiful.

"I'm sorry." He couldn't have been more surprised than she looked. She opened her mouth, but before she could utter a single word, he cut in. "We leave within the hour."

Her gaze drifted toward the loch where the pink and purple hues of dawn kissed the water's edge.

"I'll be ready," she whispered.

Malcolm hated to see her looking so broken and forlorn. He stepped forward, catching himself at the last minute when he wanted to touch her. "Aye," he muttered. She had to be starving having eaten none of the food she'd chucked at him the night before. "Come break your fast."

Rose followed him toward the camp where the men were already breaking down the tents. He grabbed a bannock from a stack on a log and handed it to her. She nibbled at it like a mouse. He stuffed one into his mouth to keep from telling her he thought she looked beautiful.

When she was finished, he led her silently to the loch to wash up and then she requested the bush for privacy. He kept well away, but not too far so that he couldn't hear if she chose to run away, or befell some accident. Then he lifted her onto his horse, climbed behind and gave the order to move out.

An hour had passed in silence, when Rose asked, "Why did ye say ye were sorry?"

Malcolm shrugged. "Because I was."

She tilted her head back, glancing at him. "For the binds?"

He met her gaze for just a split-second. How could he tell her he was sorry for having to take her at all? "Aye."

Rose's gaze returned to the road. "When will we be at Kildrummy?"

"'Haps three more days." Malcolm scanned the woods to their left, squinting his eyes when he saw movement and then only too relieved to see that it was simply a doe and her fawn.

"And my son?"

He grunted. "Same."

"Sir!" The shout came from a young warrior who rode quickly to Malcolm's side. "We've spotted something behind us, sir."

Malcolm was instantly on alert. "What is it?"

The lad's eyes shifted to the lady then back. "*Them.*"

Mackenzies. Had to be.

Malcolm signaled to Kavan to take Rose, effortlessly lifting her off his lap and plopping her on Kavan's. A twinge of jealousy tried to niggle its way inside him, but he forced it away. There was no time, nor any reason, for it. More important things were at hand.

"Show me," he said to the scout.

Malcolm followed the lad to the end of their caravan, and then past, 'haps a mile back, overlooking a ridge. In the distance, he could see an army of warriors coming their way. They did indeed look to be wearing Mackenzie colors. *Ballocks!*

"We'll need to pick up our pace. At the rate they are riding, they will catch up to us soon."

Malcolm and his guard hurried back to the caravan. He pulled up alongside Kavan, and warned of the Mackenzies that followed, then shifted Rose back into his lap. Instantly feeling the heat of her body seeping into his. A sense of rightness and comfort made him stiffen.

"What is happening?" she asked.

Grinding his teeth, he considered sharing with her what he'd seen. However, he decided against it. It would only worry her and the lady was already tense enough.

"'Tis nothing, we simply need to move more quickly."

"I dinna believe ye."

Malcolm dragged in a breath, not having the energy to spar with her when he needed to concentrate on keeping her safe. "We are being followed."

"By who?"

He didn't answer; instead he kicked his horse into a quicker pace, concentrating on the road ahead, the woods beside them, the location of the sun and the breathing of his mount. He prayed Lucifer could make it to the end of the day at this pace, else the beast would suffer, and Malcolm would never forgive himself for injuring the animal.

Rose's warm hand slid over his forearm. "Please, Montgomery, tell me."

He always was weak when it came to a woman, especially hearing them beg. "We are being followed by Mackenzies."

Her sharp indrawn breath cut through the morning air. Then, with a voice filled with joy, she said, "He has come to rescue me."

Malcolm gritted his teeth and resisted the urge to hold her tighter, to tell him that she would never belong to anyone else but him. "Lass, I daresay, Mackenzie will not be rescuing ye at all."

"Because ye won't let him." Her tone was petulant, and she crossed her arms over her chest.

How sad it was that Rose truly had no idea the man she'd thought to marry, to make an alliance with, did not care for her at all. "Because he does not care if ye live, lass. He wants your land, and the ink is already dry on the parchment. 'Tis but a trifle if ye dinna live. Do ye know how easy it would be for him to bribe a priest to tell the king he wed the two of ye in secret?"

The woman stiffened before him, and he knew he'd said something hurtful, but it was the truth. She deserved that much.

"I will let the king tell ye everything," he added.

"I want ye to tell me. And I want ye to tell me now." Her voice wavered with anger, hurt.

Malcolm dragged in a breath, searching for patience even though he wasn't entirely certain he'd be able to find it. "Look, lass, I understand ye're scared, that ye dinna entirely trust me. But I need ye, too. I beg ye to trust me. We canna stop. Not while I'm trying to save your life, lass. I need to concentrate on riding up through these mountains and not on the bastards who follow. I know what their intentions are and that will have be enough for ye to believe."

"I canna! I won't!"

Malcolm let out a deep sigh. "Please. For the sake of your child, believe me."

"My son... Sweet, Jesu, Montgomery, will he go after my son?"

The lady started to shake, her fear flowing through him. Blast it, but Malcolm hated to be the one to have caused her such fear. Well, dammit, he wasn't! It was all Mackenzie's fault, and soon enough she'd see the right of it.

With one hand on the reins and the other wrapped tight around her waist, he urged Lucifer into a faster run. Come hell or high water, he was going to keep her safe and out of the hands of the man who had manipulated his way into a marriage bargain with her.

"He'll think your son is with us, my lady. That was why we routed him differently."

"I dinna know who to trust." Her voice quavered, and she leaned forward, as though trying to put distance between them, but a leap of the horse over a small dip in the earth forced her back into him.

Malcolm breathed in deep, soaking up her lavender scent. "Ye can trust me, my lady."

Letting go of her waist, he reached for the ruby dagger at his waist. "Open your hand," he said.

Rose tilted her head back to look up at him.

"Open it," he urged.

She held out her hand, fingers stretched. Malcolm placed the hilt of the dagger against the flat of her palm and closed her fingers around it, his own hand still cocooning hers.

"I, Sir Malcolm Montgomery, swear to ye, Rose Munro, Lady of Foulis Castle, that ye and your son have my protection. If for any reason I should go against ye, I vow to lay still as ye drive this dagger into my heart."

Her fingers trembled beneath his, and he tightened his grasp over her hand, hoping to impart strength.

"I canna take this," she said. "Your vow means much to me, and I shall remember it, but this dagger—"

"Is yours."

She shook her head, her soft hair tickling his chin. "Where did ye get it?"

"The king. He gave it to me in exchange for my service. The dagger once belonged to King Richard the Lionheart."

"Our king thinks much of ye to give ye such a priceless gift."

Malcolm's chest swelled with pride. "Aye, my lady. I have earned our king's trust. Just as I hope to earn yours."

"I trust ye, Sir Malcolm, because I've no other choice." Rose slipped her hand from his, the dagger still held tight in her grasp. Her gaze was fixed on the blade, but for some reason he did not fear that she might use it on him.

Malcolm wasn't prepared for how her words would affect him. Gaining her trust had not been part of the deal. Had not been something required in stealing her away from her betrothed and delivering her to the king. And forced trust was not trust at all, even if it would make his task all the easier.

And made him feel like a complete and utter cad. He'd tied her up the night before for heaven's sake. He deserved a dagger to the heart at the way he'd treated her.

"Trust isn't simply given, my lady, it must be earned, and I vow to earn yours wholly." He returned the dagger to her hand. "Keep this as a promise."

"My thanks, sir," she murmured, her voice thick.

He could guess she was close to tears.

"Call me Malcolm, please."

She shook her head, the top of her head scraping beneath his chin "'Tis not proper for us to call each other by our birth names."

"I'd not call our situation proper at all, my lady."

"Then I must insist ye call me Rose when we are alone, as we are now." She tucked the jeweled dagger into the leather belt at her waist.

"Rest assured, I will maintain propriety in the presence of others."

The same scout that had ridden forward before, appeared once more. "Sir, they are gaining on us."

"Damn," Malcolm muttered.

Mackenzie was a brutal man, he'd likely not even attempt to negotiate, but instead would insist on a slaughter. He'd call it a battle to return his betrothed to him, but in truth, he'd simply kill Rose and then take over her lands, allowing the English to infiltrate the north.

There was only one sure way to guarantee that Munro lands stayed out of Mackenzie's hands. And that was a solution he was not willing to explore—and it wasn't even foolproof if

Malcolm got killed. *Marriage.* He'd bypassed thirty-six years of his life without so much as a brush with the kirk and marriage vows. He'd be damned if he was going to take that leap now.

Och, but the thought of marriage... Another whiff of lavender and her supple backside pressed to his groin had him thinking that perhaps marriage wasn't such a bad idea. He could still feel the soft way her lips had brushed his. The way her cheeks heated when she argued and the fearless way she stood up to him. Malcolm hadn't found a woman he respected so much in a long time.

Well, it wasn't possible to marry her between now and when the Mackenzies reached them. And jutting up on their right was a much easier solution for the time being—the Cairngorm Mountains. The journey would be treacherous, but it would slow down the advancing enemies and it would get them to Kildrummy faster.

Malcolm glanced sideways at his scout. "Inform the men we will ride up into the mountains."

The scout's mouth fell open. There was more than just the treacherous terrain in the Cairngorms, there were outlaws, wild animals and spirits to contend with.

A stern look from Malcolm and the scout turned around to give the orders.

He urged his mount right, climbing up into the mountains, where the grounds were uneven with rock and tree roots, making the going slower. Lucifer had traversed these lands before and knew what was expected of him.

Malcolm held up his arm, blocking branches from whipping against their cheeks as they went. His men came along steadily and as quietly as they could behind them. Thank the saints the spring rains had yet to start, soaking the ground and making it impossible to maneuver through slick brush, leaving a trail of tracks for their enemies to follow.

Aye, the mountains were dangerous, but in this case, he'd take peril over a lifetime of marriage.

Hmmm...

If that were so, why did he wrap his arm around Rose, if only to feel her warmth against his abdomen?

5

Their pace was slow and grueling up the steep mountains. More than once Malcolm's horse faltered in his footing. Each time, the warrior's grasp on Rose tightened, to the point where she barely had to hold on, and the feel of his arm around her made her feel safe, warm and... not like a captive.

His vow of protection, that he would die if he betrayed her, came back to Rose in whispered waves every so often as the hours passed. Who was this man, and how could he so readily be willing to die for her? Aye, there did appear to be some sort of connection between the two of them, a spiritual melding, or perhaps it was only nerves, but it couldn't be discounted even if they barely knew one another.

She barely knew Mackenzie either, but she'd never felt anything for him other than the stark truth that she had to wed him. Rose chewed her lip. Well, maybe that wasn't exactly true. She knew more about the man than she was willing to admit. He imbibed in whisky quite a bit more than most men. And when he was imbibing, he tended to be on the angrier side. At least from what she remembered when she'd seen him at the betrothal negotiation. He'd not spoken to her, in fact seemed to avoid her mostly. And the rumors from his men were that he still liked to go raiding. They'd agreed on a wedding date the following month—just a week after she was abducted by Malcolm.

More disturbingly was the clause that had been added to their betrothal contract giving him guardianship over the young Laird Munro, her son, in the event she died before they could be wed. A clause that she had readily accepted wanting her son and their clan to be protected from the English. She couldn't expect Myra and Daniel to protect her forever.

Had she signed away her life—and the life of her son—to a madman?

If it was the truth that the king had sent Malcolm to capture her, his duty of seizing her did not extend to loyalty. So why did he want hers and why did he vow it in return?

Because she had to. Because she needed to.

Furthermore, why was she becoming used to the idea of him being her protector, rather than the opposite? The feel of his arms around her... the touch of his lips... his lopsided grin... his intense gaze... The way he so readily asked for her trust and vowed his protection of her.

She wanted to.

According to the scout, the Mackenzies had not followed them up the rise, perhaps not thinking they'd have gone to the trouble. Thank the saints that was the case. She only hoped they didn't realize that her son had been put on a different route.

If her son were lost to her...

Rose shook her head. She couldn't even fathom it.

The sounds of a waterfall ahead broke through the subtle breezes. Birds tittered as they sought to find their nests. Gloaming was quick approaching, turning the skies dusky, and soon, when summer arrived, the fireflies would make swirls of glowing light, her son's favorite time of day.

"We'll make camp by the falls," Malcolm ordered.

Rose blew out a sigh of relief. The mountains were hazardous in daylight, but even more so at night. They'd been lucky to make it this far unscathed. She scanned the landscape for signs of the falls, not seeing them up close just yet. The air grew cooler as the sun began to settle into the horizon. Rose could hear the sound of water rushing, tumbling in on itself and she waited for the faint spray to touch her skin, signaling they were near, but nothing yet.

Malcolm's horse came close to a ridge, and there it was, the subtle splash of water. She glanced toward the rise above them, watching the water fall in graceful waves.

"Where does it come from?" Certainly there wasn't a loch or river at the top of the mountain.

"As Beltane approaches, the mountain ice caps melt creating falls."

Rose shivered. "I wager the water is frigid."

"Aye," Malcolm said with a chuckle. "And refreshing." He led his horse through the trees, picking their way down the rise until they came to the bank of what the mountain had created into its own small sound.

The men were dismounting, and started to set up camp as they had the night before. None of them talked to her. Most avoided her gaze, though they did set up her tent, filled with blankets, close to the fire to keep her warm.

"My lady," Malcolm said, climbing down and then reaching a hand to her.

Whereas the day before, Rose had been insistent on getting down herself, today she was more grateful for his assistance. Her muscles were sore and she was exhausted. A part of her resistance toward him was melting. The more she thought about Mackenzie, what she'd heard and witnessed the more inclined she was to believe Malcolm. He was taking her straight to the king.

"Do ye think we are safe here?" she asked, her mind on Mackenzie, wondering how she'd not seen through him before—but knowing, she'd not have tried. She wanted her clan to be safe. She knew Mackenzie to be a dispassionate man, cunning even. She'd not thought she'd be in danger, but she did worry over whether or not he'd treat her with respect. He'd barely spoken two words to her during their betrothal negotiations.

"For now. I'll send out scouts and have the men stand guard. No one will harm ye, of that ye have my word."

Rose nodded and followed Malcolm to a bush, as was their usual ritual when stopping. When she was done he led her to her tent.

"Why do ye not rest awhile inside? I'll have one of the men bring ye something to eat."

The pile of blankets certain to be inside the tent called to her for both the warmth and comfort they'd provide, and yet, she didn't want to be alone.

"Will ye eat with me?" she asked.

Malcolm's face darkened, his eyes scanning her from her head to her toes. Rose couldn't help but feel exposed, and rather than try to cover herself, she stretched to her full height, basking in his perusal. Oh dear heavens, what was she about? As soon as she realized what she was doing, she crossed her arms over her chest in silent protection. She might have enjoyed his kiss, but that did not mean she could invite him into her bed.

"I canna," he finally said.

Disappointment filled her. "Good night, then," she said quietly.

Malcolm gazed at her a moment longer, then nodded briskly before turning and walking away.

Perhaps an hour or so later, Rose emerged from her tent, full on a hunk of roasted rabbit and a fair share of warmed ale. Though she was physically exhausted, her mind reeled, and she thought to wash by the sound, in hopes of clearing her thoughts and then going to bed. A cursory glance around the camp did not show Malcolm to be in sight. Where had he gone?

Wrapping a blanket around her shoulders, she approached Kavan who sat before a small fire drinking from a mug.

"Where is Montgomery?" she asked.

Kavan glanced up at her and shrugged. "He said ye were to stay in your tent."

Rose bit her lip and nodded. She needed to ask him the question she'd been worried over for the past two days. "Did ye kill my men?"

Kavan glanced up at her sharply, his eyes assessing. "Nay, my lady."

A lie? He looked to be telling the truth. "Why?"

The warrior returned his attention to his mug. "We were not sent to kill them. Go back to your tent."

Rose ignored his demand. "Did ye injure them?"

Kavan sighed, the long kind of sigh someone made when they were being thoroughly pestered and could do naught about it. "Nothing life threatening."

Rose breathed out a sigh of relief. "Did they follow?"

Kavan glanced at the ground. "No, my lady."

"Why?"

He took a long sip from his cup, wiping the excess from his mouth with the back of his hand. "Because, we warned them of the attack on the castle containing their young laird, that if they followed, both of ye would die."

Rose stood a little taller, feeling indignation take hold. "So my men were tricked?"

"I should say no more. Ye'll have to talk to Montgomery

about it. Go back to your tent and I'll have him come and speak with ye."

"Rest assured, I will speak to him about this."

Kavan nodded dejectedly, as though he had hoped she would not. "Will ye please return to your tent now?"

"I will return, just as soon as I wash my hands and face at the water's edge."

Kavan shook his head. "Nay."

"Dinna be a boor, sir." Rose straightened to her full height and glowered at the man as she did to her son when he was not listening. "I am a lady and require time to tend my ablutions."

The warrior grunted and stood.

Rose held out her hand. "There is no need to follow. The water is just over there."

When he opened his mouth to argue she shook her head. "I'll not be escaping, and ye should know better. For one thing, Montgomery is in possession of my son, secondly, we are being chased by a possible madman, and thirdly, ye are taking me to see the king, are ye not?"

Kavan nodded.

Rose stepped forward and patted him on his shoulder. "Ye see? There is no reason to invade my privacy. I have no plans to escape as it will only endanger myself, my son, and ye're taking me to see the verra person I can talk to in order to escape your clutches. Go back to your cup. I will only be a moment."

He looked ready to argue with her again and rather than stay to hear what he had to say, Rose rushed toward the sound of the falls.

Dropping to her knees, ignoring the cold wet earth sinking into her gown, Rose let the blanket fall behind her. She rolled up her sleeves and plunged her hands into the frigid water. Just as icy as the mountain caps it had melted from. Bringing the cool water to her face she took a deep drink and then splashed it over her cheeks. She sat back on her heels, mesmerized by the water plunging from the top of the rise into the pool it had created on its own. The sound of it, as beautiful and majestic as it looked with the moon shining silver on it.

In the span of two days, her once simple life had become utterly complicated. A betrothal was not just a betrothal. A man she thought she could trust to keep her clan and son safe apparently would not. And a man she'd thought to be danger-ous, who in fact stole her away from her people, was not. He'd saved her. And her men had not been harmed.

Lord, she prayed that was the truth.

A splash from the center of the water jarred Rose from her thoughts. She saw no one rise up and no one at the sound's edge. Swallowing, she gazed out into the water, only lit by the light of moon and the sprinkling of golden stars.

The splashing sound came again, only closer this time. From the depths of the darkened water she watched a figure rise. Sleek and muscled. Tall and broad. All sinewy strength. Her cheeks heated. 'Twas a man. But not just any man. 'Twas Malcolm.

And he was completely nude.

Thank goodness for the darkness, else she would be able to see all of him, rather than the outline of his strong body. Yet, part of her wished for the moon to brighten just a smidge.

Rivulets of waters caught the light of the moon as they sluiced over his frame. He shook his head, and swiped a hand over his face.

He'd not yet seen her.

She could peek a little longer or slink away quietly without him ever knowing she was there.

Heat tingled its way over her limbs, tightening her belly,

warming between her thighs. Her nipples grew rigid and she had the sudden intense urge to stand up, press her body to his and kiss him. And not in the way he'd kissed her before. She wanted a hot, carnal kiss. The way her husband used to kiss her after blowing out the candle, when his hands had run over her body, hot and hungry.

And that's what she was now. Hungry. Ravenous for the touch of this man.

'Twas completely absurd, and sinful.

But it had been so long... and...

"Shall I refrain from getting dressed?" The sound of Malcolm's voice startled her, and she glanced up from where she'd been staring—at his middle—toward his face, though she couldn't make out his eyes, she could see just the faint outline of his smile.

"I... I didna see ye there," she lied, her voice catching. She leapt to her feet, fingers curling around the fabric of her skirt.

Malcolm laughed. "'Tis a trick of the light, if the sun had been out, I'm certain ye would have seen everything."

He was teasing her, taunting her for staring.

"Well, never mind that, 'tis verra improper of ye to have just stood there," she admonished.

He walked toward her; still as bare as the day he was born. "And even more improper for ye to have stared." Malcolm's voice had taken on a gravelly, heady tone.

Rose swallowed hard around the lump in her throat. "I did not... stare."

"Oh, aye, lass, ye did. I felt your eyes burning into my flesh."

Rose gasped at his words, but more so that he'd caught her red handed. She was guilty. "Why ye—"

"Tsk tsk, ye'll not be calling me any more names, will ye?"

"Ogre!" she spat, then spun on her heels, tripping over the blanket she'd forgotten that she'd let fall behind her.

But her hands and knees never hit the ground. Malcolm's strong grip clasped at her waist and he spun her around, hauling her body up against his. She gasped again, but this time at the entirely improper intimate contact. How could his body be so hot after coming out of such frigid water?

The wetness of his skin seeped into her gown. Branding her.

His body was hard, rigid lines. One hand settled firmly at the base of her spine, the other slid to her rear, cupping her and lifting her slightly. Hips pressed to hers, and between them... A length of flesh that could have been stone, cradled at the throbbing place between her thighs.

"Malcolm," she breathed out with mock outrage, then clasped her lips closed, swallowing around the nervous lump in her throat. If he didn't kiss her soon, she'd have to kiss him herself, if only to get the urgent need out of her system.

"Och, Rose, but has anyone ever told ye what a gem ye are?"

She nodded, licked her lips. Let her hands tentatively press to the corded muscles of his upper arms. Pure strength. Pure heat. Pure, rippling brawn... She squeezed, stroked, just a little bit, curiosity taking precedence over her mind telling her to behave.

"Do ye know what I like to do with gems?" he whispered, his mouth so close to hers that she could feel his breath on her lips.

"Put them in daggers?" She stroked the sinew of his arms, her breaths coming fast, her heartbeat even faster.

Malcolm chuckled with sensual ease. "Cherish them. Study them. Touch them."

Rose ceased to breathe as with an aching slowness, his lips descended toward hers.

❧ 6 ❧

For the love of all that was holy, why was Malcolm kissing the lass? Especially while he was completely nude.

The feel of her curves pressed to the hard lines of his body... Malcolm deepened the kiss. His entire body demanding satisfaction. The hardness of his cock probing the folds of her gown, seeking out the folds at the apex of her thighs.

He was a cad. Taking advantage of her willingness to kiss him... Yet, he couldn't stop. And she wasn't pushing him away either.

Her lips were sweet as honey, her skin as smooth as the freshest cream. Lord help him... The need to feel her lips on his had been practically uncontrollable since the moment, that first time, he'd pushed his hasty lips to hers. Never mind that what he was doing was completely inappropriate, or that it brought to mind the fact that he was thirty-five and still had to marry and here was a warm, willing, beautiful lass in need of marrying.

Malcolm had boasted of his freedom to every man he knew who tied the knot with a woman. He was a free man. Free to do as he wished. Free to forgo roots and a household. Free to bed whom he pleased—and yet, he didn't.

Aye, his willingness to please his king and do as the Royal Council bid was highly praised as was his ability to see his missions through not only in a timely manner but one in which impressed his sovereign. But kissing Rose... Feeling her fingers curling against the muscles of his shoulders... That was something he'd wanted and missed. And he'd not even known it until now.

He'd been so busy warring, politicking and celebrating to take into consideration what life would be like outside of those things. What it would be like to lay down roots and allow his heart to open to a woman.

There had been a time, years before, when he'd been left in charge of Glasgow Castle while his brother, Jamie, went north on a mission for the council. He'd found the entire ordeal to be distasteful, even though he'd done it well. Funny thing was, when his brother returned home and a wife shortly followed, Jamie had gladly given up his position with the Royal Council to Malcolm so he could stay home with his wife, Lorna, his soon-to-be born bairn and to run his lands and clans.

Blast it all, his brother wasn't even bored. In fact, Jamie still battled some, and then had a warm, loving lass to go home to—along with a brood of children.

Malcolm groaned, a soft whimper of a reply greeted his ears like a blessed echo.

If not for their camp a few dozen paces away, he'd lay her down on the forest floor and make good on the promise of his kiss and the pulsing arousal scorching his limbs.

Rose's fingers slid from their perch on his shoulders down

to his chest where his heart pounded against his ribs. He clutched her closer. Rose was no quivering virgin, but a woman full of passion, and judging from the way she kissed him, she enjoyed pleasures of the flesh.

"Och, lass, ye could tempt an angel to sin..." He sucked gently at her lower lip. "I want ye more than I've ever wanted another."

But those must not have been the right words to say, or what she wanted to hear, for suddenly she broke their kiss and shoved him away. Stumbling back a few feet, she wiped at her lips with the back of her hand, as though disgusted.

Malcolm frowned, not certain if he should be offended or concerned or both.

Rose shook her head vehemently. "Nay. I canna!"

Malcolm reached for her. 'Haps she simply needed reassurance. "I swear, I'll not abuse ye. 'Twould be pleasurable for the both of us."

A disgusted noise left her mouth. "Ye are too forward, warrior. I barely know ye. I'd not sully the memory of my lawful husband, God rest his soul, by bedding down with a man who has taken me captive and put my son's life at risk! I'd not bed down with any man I was not lawfully wedded to. How dare ye suggest I engage in such immoral acts? Ye're lucky I didna pull out the pretty dagger ye gave me."

Malcolm's frown deepened, suddenly feeling very exposed in his naked state. Had she not enjoyed the kiss? She'd not pushed him away. Actually, she'd touched him, explored. Moaned. She liked it whether she wanted to admit it or not, but Malcolm wasn't going to argue that with her.

"My lady," he said softly, keeping his hands at his sides. "I meant no offense, and I'd not deem what we have shared, nor what we could share, as immoral. 'Tis the truth that I've taken a fancy to ye, and I got carried away by your kiss."

"Ye do seem apt to kiss me a lot," she mused.

Was she complaining? He couldn't tell. It sounded more like a question, rather than a statement.

"I confess, I canna help it."

"Do ye go around kissing a lot of women? Does it keep them subdued while ye steal them away?" She sounded a little miffed and he couldn't help but wonder if there was a slight twinge of jealousy in her tone.

"I swear I dinna go around kissing lasses. 'Tis a fact, ye are the first I've kissed in a long time." Why did he feel the need to confess such to her?

She was silent a moment long enough that he was ready to suggest she return to camp while he find his clothes. But then she broke the silence.

"I have not kissed anyone since my husband died nine years ago."

Malcolm felt like he'd been punched in the gut. He was even more of a cad than he thought. Here she was a pious woman, keeping the memory of her husband alive in her mind and he'd just taken over the last kiss she'd remember having.

"I'm sorry for your loss, my lady."

An audible sigh escaped her lips. "'Twas not ye who is to blame for his passing."

"I know it, but I feel the need to convey my condolences to ye on the loss of your husband, and that I kissed ye without your permission."

"Thank ye," she said quietly. "Your kiss was not as bad as I made it out to be. I..."

Malcolm stepped closer to her, wanting to reach out his hand to her, but holding himself back. "Tell me," he prodded gently.

"I fear I am most displeased with myself."

"Why?"

"Because I liked it." She sounded heartbroken. "Because while my son is somewhere in the wilds of the Highlands, unsafe, I am allowing a man to kiss me."

"Your son is safe."

"Ye keep saying that, but how can ye be certain? *We* are not even safe."

"We are. I promise, no harm will come to either of ye. I gave ye my vow. My men will protect your son. The lad is in the very best of the king's men's care. He'll not want for anything, save his mother's company which I aim to provide him."

"I have to trust ye in that, because there is no other option. Even though ye told me trust has to be earned... I canna think what would happen if I didna."

Malcolm nodded, though he wasn't sure she could see. "Would ye really have pulled King Richard's dagger on me?"

She let out a great sigh. "As mad as it sounds, I dinna feel unsafe with ye, but I am terrified for my child. He is all I have." Her voice caught on a sob.

"Ye will be reunited with him soon."

"Tell me why ye took us. Please, Malcolm, I beg ye. I need to know."

The muscle in Malcolm's jaw clenched. He really ought to let the king tell her, but given that he stood before her naked, having just kissed her with enough fire to ignite the forest around them, he supposed he owed her that much.

"Let me gather my clothes, and then I will tell ye everything."

Rose laughed, a light, tinkling sound. "I had forgotten ye were without them."

"That makes only one of us."

Rose followed him back to the water's edge, and he pulled on his shirt, pleated his plaid and laid on the bank, rolling it around his hips and belting it into place. He pulled on his hose and boots, and then swung the extra fabric of his plaid onto his shoulder, pinning in place with the dragon brooch passed down to him by his grandfather.

The lass settled beside him, her sweet floral scent wrapping around him. Malcolm breathed in deep, fisting his hands to keep from touching her.

"The king sent me to gather ye and your son. But we had to do so in a way that looked as though ye were abducted. Ye see, the thing is, Cathal Mackenzie is a traitor."

Rose gasped, her hand fluttering to touch her neck. "A traitor? Nay, 'tis impossible! Why would Daniel and Myra betroth me to a traitor?"

"My gut tells me they didna know." Malcolm cut himself off before saying more.

Suspicion was not lost on her. "Why do I feel there is a *but* added to that?"

"Because, lass, I'm afraid there is. While my gut and your word says they are true to the king, there is still the matter of the contract with the Mackenzie."

"How do ye know he's a traitor?"

"The bastard is suspected of siding with the English. Our king has intercepted communications between Mackenzie and suspected traitors. He planned to marry ye and take control of the waterways Munro lands surround. He could then allow the English to moor their boats and invade the Highlands with more ease."

Rose gasped. "Nay!" But then she recalled that after the betrothal papers were signed, Cathal had suddenly disappeared. Ridden off with his men. A maid had sworn she'd seen a small English garrison outside the walls that had ridden away with Cathal, but the maid had also been overly drunk on ale.

"Aye."

She jumped up, pacing before him. Oh, how they should have listened! But it was Rose who insisted the maid had lied. A woman who'd been jealous of her since she'd arrived there over a decade before and 'taken' Byron away from her. "Daniel would not have known of this. He would not have gone against the king. He fought beside William Wallace; they were cousins!"

"I know it."

She stopped a minute, staring in his direction. "Does King Robert know it?"

"Aye. Though he wishes to question Daniel Murray, he is more inclined to believe the man is innocent. What did ye stand to gain from an alliance with Mackenzie?"

"Protection." She resumed her pacing. "Our lands border the Ross clan. They've been the enemies of our clan for years. Their old laird killed my husband."

Made sense. They did need protection from their enemies. "But why did ye wait until now to marry when ye've needed protection for so much longer?"

"They left us in peace for some time, but as of late, they've been raiding again. They canna be trusted, and many in our clan were killed when they attacked us years ago. We have yet to replenish our men. We have help from our allies— Daniel's men—but I cannot keep his men with me forever, he needs them for himself, and his generosity I'll never be able to repay. It was time. I thought for my son, for his sake, that it would be best to marry into a strong clan that could keep him safe. Provide him with a leader that he could follow and learn from, that would show him how to be a laird when his day comes. Mackenzie lands border ours, and when Cathal approached about an alliance by marriage, I asked Daniel to help." Her hands came to press at her cheeks. "Oh, nay... This is all my fault."

Malcolm shook his head and reached for her hands,

pulling them from her face and wrapping them in his grip. Her fingers were cold and trembling. "Nay, lass. None of this is your fault. Ye were only doing what ye thought best for your son."

"Do ye not see, Malcolm? In doing so, I have put him at risk."

From the moment she felt her bairn quicken within her belly, Rose had been determined to keep him safe. And it would seem, though he started this life in less than favorable conditions, downright heinous, in fact, she had, until recently, done all she could to keep him well and protected.

How could she have been so stupid? How could she not have realized. All the clues in her mind coming together at once. She should have seen, but she'd been blind to the prospects, dead set on her goal of protecting her clan she'd failed to see that the enemy was right in front of her.

The idea that her betrothal to Cathal Mackenzie now meant her son could possibly be in mortal danger was more than she could bear. Aye, Malcolm had not said as much, but Rose knew. If Cathal was only seeking to marry her so he could gain access to the shores, then what did he need with a young lad who could grow up to be laird one day and challenge him. The answer was simple and terrifying.

Nothing.

This was why the king had sent his prized warrior after her.

Because they knew that she and Byron were in mortal danger, and the only way to draw the beast out into the open was to make them the bait.

Oh, she knew that wasn't exactly what the king and Malcolm had set out to do. They had stolen her and her child under the pretense of safety, but they were still the lure for the beast that wanted to gobble them up.

Barely able to sleep after figuring out the notion, and not able to even take a bite of the sweet bannock given her that morning, Rose sat before Malcolm on his great black steed, the swaying motion lulling her into sleep, only to be jarred back awake by the fears running through her mind like a pack of ferocious wolves.

This time when she jerked her head up, she bumped into Malcolm's chin. He grunted and leaned down to whisper, his lips touching her ear. "Rest, my lady. We've a ways to go yet."

She shivered, fingers of desire warring with her fists of indignation.

Even though spring had nearly arrived, there was a bite to the air that left her chilled. The gooseflesh covering her skin had nothing to do, whatsoever, with the man whose lap she sat upon. And she'd swear that on the Bible, if only to later pay a penance.

"I canna," she said, her voice sounding far away over the rumbling of the horse's hooves echoing the beat of her heart.

"I know ye worry over your lad, but the best thing ye can do is rest so ye've the energy to keep up with him when we arrive at Kildrummy. There's certain to be a number of things a young excitable lad is wanting to chase and discover."

"We still have at least two days to travel. I can sleep later," she grumbled, not wanting to agree, even though what he said made sense.

"Suit yourself, but my chin would thank ye if ye rested a little bit and stopped your head bobbing."

Rose laughed, sinking back against Malcolm's warm body, forcing herself not to recall to mind his fervent and heated kisses, the length of his strong, hard body.

"That's it," he murmured. "Sleep."

She had half a mind to argue with him, to remind him she didn't take orders, but her eyes drifted closed and the rocking of the horse combined with the heat of his body and her exhaustion proved too much.

Rose drifted in and out of sleep the rest of the day, vaguely waking when they took a break at noon to relieve the horses and themselves. As soon as her backside was planted between Malcolm's thighs on the horse, she was once again sleeping. By the time the sun started its slow ebb to the horizon, they commenced a search for camp along a river. The burble of water and the whisper of the wind against the reeds was enough of a lullaby to send her back into a deep sleep, but the rumble of her stomach reminded Rose she'd hardly eaten since the day before.

As much as she hated to admit it, Malcolm was right that she needed to take care of herself, else, she wouldn't be any good to her son when they were reunited. And they would be.

They passed quietly by a small village, Malcolm warning not to alert the crofters who resided there else they give away the information to Mackenzie should he come looking for them. They'd lost him on the rise, but it was only a matter of time before he tracked them down again.

About two or three miles down river from the village, the waning sun lit upon what looked to be an abandoned croft. The door hung askew on a hinge, and the roof had more than a couple of holes in the thatch. Brown, sagging weeds and grass grew high against the wattle and daub building, giving the appearance that when the fauna had flourished the previous summer, no one had been there to tame it back.

"Kavan, take two men and check the building. We might just have a shelter this night for the lady."

Rose sat up a little straighter. Was it too much to hope that there was a bed inside the croft? A little beating with a stick and she might be able to sleep on a straw mattress. Wishful thinking. Lord, she was spoiled to be thinking of such comforts at a time like this.

The men approached the building with their swords drawn. From atop his horse, Kavan nudged the door with his foot, revealing a dark and empty room. The two other warriors jumped down from their horses and made their way inside while Kavan rode his horse around the back, perhaps to catch anyone who might have escaped that way somehow.

A moment later, the two warriors and Kavan returned to the front of the croft and gave the signal that all was quiet.

"A roof for ye, my lady," Malcolm said.

She hoped her smile conveyed her pleasure. "And I'd never thought to be so grateful for one."

"Come, let us get ye situated and then I shall tame that rumbling belly."

Rose flushed with embarrassment.

Malcolm dismounted behind her, then reached up, taking her in his arms, before depositing her too quickly onto the ground. Though Rose was becoming used to the way his hands felt on her waist, and his arms around her while they rode together, each time the sensation only seemed to build upon her already enflamed awareness. A familiar guilt needled its way into her thoughts and she tried to reason with it—with her demons.

She was prepared to marry another man—a traitor if Malcolm was to be believed. That was more of an insult to her beloved husband's memory than a few stolen kisses with a man who, though his actions were a bit misguided, was trying to keep her safe. As soon as they arrived at Kildrummy, she'd seek out the kirk and confess her sinful thoughts, and pray for the safety of her son. Then perhaps, whatever it was that had seemed to take hold of her would be rushed away like debris on a current.

Inside the croft, the men had gathered a few broken chairs and buckets and put them over the small hearth, lighting a fire. Despite the small dwelling's tumbled look, as though someone had recently ransacked the place, it was kind of cozy.

"Come, I'll give ye a few minutes to wash by the river," Malcolm said.

Rose followed, taking the proffered plaid and a small ball of soap.

"'Tis not anything as luxurious as ye might be used to, but 'twill get the job done," he said with a tantalizing smile, as though he recalled how vividly she'd studied him the night before.

"Aye. This is all I need. My gratitude to ye." She couldn't wait to freshen up. Already her skin was tingling with expectation of a good scrubbing.

While Malcolm stood guard, his back to her, Rose stripped down to her chemise—too anxious to undress completely in the wilderness, then realizing she didn't have a change of clothes, forced herself to remove that, too, else she put clothes over a freezing and soaking wet chemise. She hurriedly washed, careful to check over her shoulder that he wasn't watching. She worked quickly, feeling refreshed and clean and much better smelling.

After washing, she stared at his broad back, realizing that if she were to emerge from the water, her chemise would be clear as the sky and stuck to her like a second skin. Chewing her lip a long time, she finally rushed from the water and grabbed her clothes, holding them flush to her body.

"Dinna look," she demanded.

Malcolm's shoulders shook. Was he laughing? "I'd not dare."

Rose tugged on her chemise and gown, tightening the laces and her belt, in what probably served as the fastest she'd ever gotten dressed.

"I'm done now."

Malcolm slowly swiveled toward her, a twinkle in his eye and a slight curl to his lips that made her wonder if he had in fact peeked.

"What?" she asked, suspicion rising in her tone.

"I could have peeked as ye did last night, but I'll have ye know I was a perfect gentleman." He preened before her, obviously proud to have allowed her privacy.

"Och, but ye should have, if only to get me back," she teased, wondering just where this bold woman was coming from. Never would she jest with just anyone like this. "I might have pretended not to notice, but alas, ye have missed your chance."

"Well..." he drawled. "I might have taken just the tiniest peek."

Rose's mouth fell open in mock outrage. "Ye didna."

"I did. I might have taken note of the tiny roses embroidered on the hem of your chemise."

Rose playfully smacked his arm. "Ye're a rogue, ye know that, Malcolm?"

"Aye," he laughed, the sound rich and smooth. "But as ye said, I was only paying ye back for your intrusion on my nightly swim."

"Intrusion?" Her brows danced upward. "Ha! Ye were baring your goods for the world to see."

"Baring my goods?" He chuckled heartily. "Ye do make me laugh."

Rose pretended she was indignant, raising her chin and pouting. "Well, I daresay, I'll not ask ye to escort me again. Perhaps Kavan would be a better choice." She watched from the side of her eye as he frowned at that, which of course, only made *her* smile broaden.

When they returned to the croft, the scents of cooking made Rose's belly grumble anew. The cauldron had been rinsed in the river and Kavan, despite his masculine demeanor, was chopping a few cloves of wild garlic, some onions and roots the men had found.

"I can help," Rose said, though she hadn't the slightest clue how to cook. She could barely boil water. Nevertheless, she'd not have them thinking she was not willing. "What are ye making?"

"I'm afraid if the lads dinna return with a rabbit or two, we'll be soaking some of the jerky in the stew," Kavan said.

"Maybe a boot or two," Malcolm teased.

Rose gaped in shock until she realized he was teasing.

"Funny." She rolled her eyes to the ceiling. "Shall I cut the vegetables?"

"If ye like. I've got a few spices in my satchel. 'Haps ye can tell me which ye think is best?"

Rose smiled timidly, but nodded all the same.

Kavan handed her a packet of herbs and then disappeared to hunt.

She'd done plenty of herb picking in the castle garden, as she always took an active position in her household, but she hadn't the slightest clue about what went into making stew... She knew thyme was good in soups and stews. Cinnamon was good for stewed pears, peaches and apples. Even delicious sprinkled on oats and pie. Dill was good on fish. Saffron was good on ham, and fish. Basil was good on most things. Aye, she could ask for spices all day long, and pair them. It was what they looked like she'd not much paid attention to. She supposed she might be able to guess by their scents.

Rose set to chopping a turnip using the blade Kavan had left on the table. But the first piece she cut into sent the other half flying across the small croft and hitting Malcolm square in the back of his head.

She gasped, dropped the knife, eyes wide, and covered her mouth with her hands. "I'm so sorry," she said behind her hands, muffling her voice, and hoping he couldn't hear the laughter in her pitch.

Malcolm touched the back of his head and turned to face her, his forehead wrinkled in question. "Did ye just throw something at me?"

Rose couldn't help erupting into laughter. "'Twas a bit of turnip."

He looked at her like she'd gone mad. "Why did ye throw it?"

Now she was laughing in earnest, her hands falling from her face and holding her belly. "I didna throw it, ye buffoon, it flew off the knife."

"Turnips dinna simply fly off knives." Malcolm picked up the offending vegetable and brought it toward her. "Have ye done much cutting afore?"

"Oh, aye, plenty of times," Rose said, nodding emphatically. She dusted off the turnip and set it back on the table. "Let us keep that little slip between the two of us." She gave him a wink and this time when she cut into the turnip she did it a little slower.

When nothing went flying she considered that a battle won.

Except, the moment Kavan returned, calling out that he'd brought the herbs, so startled was she, that another turnip went whizzing into the air. Malcolm, reflexes quick, caught it before it hit Kavan in the face.

"A little excited, are we not?" Kavan smirked.

Rose gave a little half-laugh, feeling her cheeks heat with embarrassment. She couldn't' be the only lady decidedly lacking in cutting skills.

"Mmhmm," Malcolm drew out. "'Haps it would be best if Lady Rose takes a look at your herbs. I think she must be exhausted from our travels."

"But she did nothing but sleep all the day," Kavan pointed out.

Rose glanced toward the ground, growing more humiliated by the second.

Coming to her rescue, Malcolm said, "Ye think she got much rest with me jostling her about?"

"True." Kavan shrugged. "I'd be much obliged if ye were to take a look at the herbs, my lady."

Rose nodded and went to examine the bundles of fresh green stems and leaves he'd tossed onto the table before returning to cutting.

Saints, but they mostly looked the same to her, though some had bigger leaves than others. The one with longer needles had to be rosemary... She picked it up and sniffed. Definitely rosemary.

"Apologies they are so crushed, but they'll still taste the same," Kavan remarked when he saw her puzzled expression.

Rose nodded, realizing the only way she'd be able to tell what they were was by scent. She'd not be a total failure after all. Lifting each bundle to her nose, she took in the earthy, succulent scents of thyme, oregano and parsley.

"I think ye can use all of these, Sir Kavan," she said.

"Truly? Each one?" His dubious expression said it all.

"Do ye not often use more than one herb in your cooking?" Likely there was a set combination of herbs that went into stew, but because she couldn't decide what they were, nor did she have the time to ponder it, else they starve, she'd supposed, why not all?

Kavan pursed his lips, frowning. "Nay, lass. My mother always only used one."

Rose smiled, happy to be helpful and to expose him to something new. "Ye can use more than one and I think ye'll find the flavoring to be much improved!"

"I like my mother's cooking," he said with a frown.

Rose blanched. "I'm sorry, I didna mean any offense."

Malcolm moved from where he'd been tending the hearth, looking ready to lay Kavan out, but then the blasted warrior chuckled.

"Just jesting with ye, my lady. Call it payback for nearly taking out my eye with a turnip. I'm always happy to improve."

❦

THE RABBIT STEW WAS SUPERB, AND HAVING EATEN TWO servings, Rose was sufficiently stuffed and tired.

"The men will camp outside, my lady, and ye can sleep in here. I'll be right outside the door should ye need me. If we wake early enough, we may reach Kildrummy by nightfall."

By tomorrow night, she could be reunited with her son. Prickles of relief skittered over her limbs

Rose studied Malcolm's handsome face, the strong angular lines, the suppleness of his lips. He was a fierce warrior, but when he looked at her, his features softened. His demeanor warmed her.

"Thank ye, Malcolm," she said, thinking how odd it was that those words should fall from her lips when just two days before she was cursing the very ground he walked on.

"Dinna thank me yet, love." He winked.

With that, he turned and left her. Her mouth was open in shock at the tender endearment, and her heart swelled. Oh, it had been so long since she'd felt tenderness from a man. And it made her crave more. Made her crave another kiss from him.

Rose fought the urge to run after him, to ask him to oblige her in a final kiss before they invariably parted the following night. Her chest tightened and a feeling close to despair tugged at her heart when she thought of never seeing him again. Then again, perhaps he would be the one to escort her and her son back to Foulis Castle when all this madness was over?

Wrapping herself in the plaid blanket he'd given her, she settled onto the straw mattress that a few of his men had beaten to within an inch of its life—leaving it not as musty or bug ridden as it probably was when they arrived. A bed! The thrill of it!

The fire in the hearth was no longer roaring, but let off enough of a glow that darkened shadows bounced on the walls of the small croft.

She'd curled up beneath the blanket and was drifting off to sleep when loud shouts startled her awake.

Sounds of complete chaos echoed from outside the croft. Were they under attack? They had to be. There was no other reason for the warning calls and the clanging of steel. Rose jumped up out of bed.

"Where is the boy?" came a roar that sounded a little like Cathal, though she'd never heard him sound so violent before.

"Safe from ye," Malcolm answered, his tone cool and chilling.

Rose was reminded of how he looked coming out of the trees when he first ambushed her party. Fierce, powerful, mystical, a supreme war machine.

"Give him to me now." Definitely Cathal.

"The only thing I'll be giving ye is the tip of my sword," Malcolm replied.

There was an unearthly cackle that sent ripples of fear over Rose's arms. Her mind hurtled back to nine years before when a similar sound had been pushed from the vile throat of Laird Ross before he killed her husband.

She had to get out of here. Cathal was a deadly adversary. Mad for blood. If he killed Malcolm, she was next, for his interest in only finding her son instead of her was not lost on Rose. The bastard couldn't give a fig about her. In all honesty, his concern for her son was mostly so he could put her lad in the ground.

Tossing aside the blanket, Rose gathered her skirts in her hands and dashed toward the back of the croft where a small window was carved into the wall near the hearth. She yanked open the shutter, relieved to see that none of Cathal's men were yet behind the croft. Taking a deep breath, she hoisted herself up only to realize she'd end up on her head in this position. Rose jumped down, retrieved a stool and climbed onto it. Gripping the shutter for balance, she put first one leg and then the other out the window.

"Where are *ye* going?" Someone grabbed her foot, yanking her the rest of the way out, her back scraping painfully on the windowsill. She fell hard to the ground, staring up into the leering face of one of Cathal's men, pain radiating through her limbs. But before he could grab her, the tip of a sword thrust through his chest from behind. His mouth opened on a silent scream and he fell to the ground beside her.

Kavan loomed where the man had once stood. "Run. Hide in the wood," he growled.

Rose ran, but she didn't stop in the woods. She ran back toward the village they'd passed. The small village would likely not have an army of its own. There was no great wall to protect them, only a slipshod fence, but perhaps some soul would take mercy on her and hide her.

The village was far. Two or three miles away. Rose's lungs burned from the exertion of running, and more than once she slipped in the dark, falling and scraping her hands on the ground.

"Please, God, help me," she whispered up to the night-time sky.

At last, she arrived at the village. She banged on one door and then another, shouting for help, but was ignored. These people would not risk their lives for a stranger.

"Lass, come now." A soft, peaceful man spoke, raising a torch, as he approached her with caution. He wore long brown woolen robes, like that of priest. "What is it ye seek?"

"My party... there was an attack..." She dropped to her knees in the middle of the road, sobbing. How would she ever get to her son now? Was she doomed to repeat her past, once more losing all she cared about?

"I am Father Henry. Come into the kirk."

Rose wiped at her tears and stood on shaky legs, taking the proffered arm of the peaceful man of God.

"All will be well," he cooed.

But Rose knew he was very, very, wrong.

8

Malcolm slammed his broadsword against Cathal's with bone-jarring force.

All around them, men clashed. The ringing of steel echoed in the night air, whipped up and carried in the wind, sounding dull in places and piercing in others. Fierce, sounds of survival bellowed from coarse throats followed by the answering screams of agony.

Through the sweat and blood dripping into Malcolm's eyes, he spotted Kavan running from around the rear of the croft and battling his way forward. Gut twisting, Malcolm knew Rose had been in danger. Even if Kavan had saved her once, she would be in danger again.

Spinning and ducking, Malcolm easily blocked the advancing blows of Cathal. The man was a fierce fighter, but he was predictable. And predictability could get a man killed. Lengthening to his full height, Malcolm attacked, connecting his sword to Cathal's. They stood unmoving, glaring at each other, and slowly Malcolm started to slide his blade along the edge of his enemy's, moving toward the hilt, showing Cathal that he, Malcolm, had superior power.

Cathal leapt back, knowing what Malcolm's signature move was. If Malcolm could get close to the hilt, he'd take control of the man's arms, bring them, along with both swords, behind Cathal's skull and moving in a crisscross swipe —a man was no longer in possession of his head.

The cur's eyes darted about, watching his men fall to Malcolm's. Not a single Montgomery man down. That was how they fought. They fought to survive. Fought to win.

Cathal started to back away.

"Ye haven't won yet," the wastrel growled. "I'm coming for the lad. He's mine. The ink is dry."

"The end of my sword is right here, why go any further?" Malcolm taunted. "Ye'll not be getting anywhere near the lad."

"Retreat!" Cathal shouted to his decrepit rabble who slowly twisted to run.

Malcolm held up his hand for his men to stay where they were, no need to chase the idiots.

Out of reach, Cathal hollered, "I'm coming for ye, Montgomery. Dinna close your eyes, else ye wake to find me bathing in your blood."

Malcolm raised a doubtful brow and chuckled. "If ye say so. Best heed your own advice, ye arsehole."

Cathal let out a savage growl, then turned on his heel and ran back into the darkened trees.

Not a breath later, Malcolm focused on the croft, while asking Kavan, "Where is Lady Rose?"

Kavan was already running toward the back of the croft and the woods beyond—opposite of where the Mackenizies retreated.

Dammit!

"Dismantle the camp!" Malcolm shouted as he leapt onto Lucifer and chased after his second. "Follow behind," he called back to them.

They had to find Rose and get the hell out of here before Cathal drank himself into thinking it was a good idea to attack again.

Malcolm caught up to Kavan, who looked frantically under every bramble and behind every tree, ripping whole branches and undoubtedly slicing into the tender flesh of his palms. "I told her to hide."

Rising trepidation soured Malcolm's stomach.

"Hell," Malcolm muttered. She could be hiding anywhere, and if they should call out to her it would only let the Mackenzie men know that she was alone and vulnerable.

"Could she have gone back to the village?" Kavan asked.

"'Tis miles from here."

"Aye."

Malcolm frowned into the darkness. He breathed in deep, hoping for even just the slightest hint of lavender to tell him she was near.

Nothing.

"I'll take half the men with me to the village," Malcolm said. "Ye continue to search."

Kavan nodded. "I'm sorry, captain. I had found her behind the croft, nearly getting sliced by a Mackenzie. I thought to send her to safety."

"Dinna weep over it, man." Malcolm's insides had twisted into something fiercer than a Celtic knot. Where was she? "Rose is tougher than she looks."

But even as he said the words, he had a hard time trusting them. His heart was pounding and the rush of battle was not ebbing but growing in strength as it streamed maddeningly through his veins.

"We'll find her," Malcolm said, then barked, "*Aller!*" to his horse.

True to form, Lucifer leapt into a run back toward camp.

Malcolm shouted orders. Half his men mounted up to follow him while the others rushed to meet Kavan.

A quarter hour later, Malcolm and his men arrived at the front of the village. All was quiet.

They walked their mounts slowly down the road, looking for any sign of life, passing one croft after another, but not even a single candle flame glowed. Even still, intuition made Malcolm stay, look further.

At the end of the road, a quaint kirk stood—a candle flame in one of its tiny windows. The building was made of stone—the only stone structure in the village, and at the top, catching the light of the moon was an iron cross.

But the candle.

That was what Malcolm couldn't stop looking at.

Why was it lit in the middle of the night, unless to draw someone near.

Himself? Or someone else?

"She's here," Malcolm said. He wasn't sure if it was the scent of lavender in the air, or the candle that beckoned to him, but he could sense Rose's presence.

Malcolm dismounted, tying the reins to the post of the kirk's fence. He checked his hands for blood, scrubbed a palm over his face and then scrubbed some more as he approached the front door. If *this*, the kirk, wasn't a sign, he wasn't sure what was.

Just the day before he'd contemplated marrying Rose for her safety. And because he desired her. Because he was drawn to her. Because she was everything he'd never known he was missing. And now, here he was, approaching a kirk with Rose inside of it.

Before he reached the door, it swung wide and an older man stepped out, his face was calm, his arms outstretched in welcome.

"What a surprise to find guests at such an hour," the man

said. His voice was congenial enough, but his eyes warily studied Malcolm and his men.

There was no invitation to come inside.

"I've come for Rose," Malcolm said.

"The roses are not yet in bloom." The priest made a good show of looking disappointed. "I'm afraid ye'll have to make do with our meager herbs, good sir."

Malcolm gritted his teeth. The vexing priest was toying with him. "Lady Rose Munro."

"I'm afraid I dinna know who ye're referring to."

"Lying is a sin," Malcolm reminded the priest.

The man nodded, his shoulders slumping slightly and the calm exterior of his face changing to one of ferocity. "God's children are protected within his walls."

"I'm not here to harm her, ye fool." Malcolm resisted stepping closer, though that took all the energy he had and his voice came out a lot harsher than he intended. "I know she's here."

The door opened wider and Rose appeared. "Sir Malcolm," she said. Her fingers, caught at her middle, grasping tightly to try to hide their trembling. "Father Henry has been kind to me."

Mo chridhe... He wanted to tug her against him and tell her all would be well, that she'd nothing to fear and he was there to keep her safe.

Malcolm locked his eyes on hers. "Ye will marry me. Now."

Her mouth fell open, and the priest immediately began to protest. Malcolm glared down at the man until he was silent, then returned his attention to Rose.

"I know 'tis not the proposal ye want. Nor perhaps am I the husband ye seek, but I promised ye protection, and your enemies are still hunting ye and your son. Marry me and I shall see that Cathal, nor any other, ever harms ye again."

Rose shifted her gaze behind Malcolm to his men that stood there. "Might we have a moment in private?" she asked.

Malcolm grunted his acceptance, and reached his hand to her. She slipped her small cold fingers against his palm, and he tucked them around his elbow, rubbing them warm as he led her down the road a few paces. He called to one of his men to retrieve Kavan and the other men from the woods so they could cease their search for Rose.

"Malcolm," she whispered urgently. "Ye dinna have to do this."

Malcolm stared down into the shadowed face of a woman he'd grown fond of over the past several days. How was it that, just like that, as quick as a snap, he'd grown to have such... what? Such intense feelings. He could not put any other name to it. But when he looked at her, his heart pounded. He wanted to hold onto her forever. To kiss her into oblivion and wake beside her each morn.

"I am five and thirty, lass. I've avoided marriage for the over a decade, I dinna take the idea of tying myself to ye until death do us part lightly."

She stiffened, and he wished he could see her expression, try to read the thoughts that would surely show on her face like a map to her soul.

"As ye said, ye've avoided it up until now, so there must be another way. I canna take from ye a life ye've hoped to lead." Her voice was void of any emotion.

Malcolm took both her hands in his. "Rose, ye're not taking anything away from me. It would be an honor to marry ye and to protect ye. It is my choice."

"But what of mine? What of my choice? Have I none?"

A trick, for in truth, she did not. Society would not allow it. But, Malcolm could show her that there were two vastly different choices she could make. "It is either me or Cathal.

Right now. Be certain ye're choosing the one who'll keep ye alive."

"And ye think ye're the lesser devil?"

Why didn't she sound assured? Suddenly, Malcolm wasn't so convinced this was a good plan, but he knew without an ounce of doubt, he was the better man. By far. "I know I'm not a traitor to my king, lass. And I'd treat ye a hell of a lot better than that bastard."

She sighed heavily, making Malcolm feel something close to uncomfortable. He didn't want to admit that she was rattling him. Women had fallen at his feet since he'd figured out how to smile to get what he wanted. But not Rose. Rose he had to work for.

"I just want my son back," she whispered.

"Ye will have him whether ye agree to marry me or not. But if the king cannot prove Cathal a traitor, there may be no other choice but to honor your betrothal, or perhaps be wed to another." Malcolm swallowed around the unusual lump in his throat. "I understand I may not be your first choice, but... Rose, I will strive to make ye happy. I will spend everyday of my life trying to prove that I'm worthy of ye."

She shook her head, and even in the dark, he could see her chewing her lip. "I dinna want to marry another. And I'd not expect ye to prove yourself worthy. Ye are worthy, Malcolm. 'Tis I that am damaged."

"Ye're as perfect a woman as I've ever met," he said softly.

Rose's grip on him tightened. "I thank ye for that, Malcolm. Truth is... I do not find ye as loathsome as ye might think." She was quiet a moment, so still he might have thought she'd fallen asleep standing up if he couldn't see the moon reflecting in her eyes. "I will marry ye."

Malcolm nodded curtly, a rush of relief escaping. "All right, then we shall have the priest perform the ceremony now. We've plenty of witnesses."

Rose was silent, but nodded her agreement.

Malcolm pulled her hand to his lips, kissing her knuckles. "I will try to make ye happy."

She shivered, and he didn't know if it was from cold, fear, or the thought of marrying him. "And I will be a dutiful wife."

"I want ye to be yourself," Malcolm said.

Rose gasped, glancing up at him, and he wished the sun had risen so he could see the expression on her face. "I shall endeavor to always be myself."

"That would please me much. And I will always be true to ye."

"Malcolm…"

"Once I say I do, ye'll be the only woman in my life—aside from my family and any daughters we might have."

"Daughters…"

"Come," he said, feeling his feet grow tingly. Was he really about to do this? Truly wed?

His brother would never believe it. His men were already staring at him as though he'd grown a second and third head. They were his trusty crew. A unit of men who thought like him. None were married, and none had any plans to do so. They liked warring and celebrating after. No woman to call them home from their fun, and no one to care if they should die.

But now, Malcolm would have a wife—and a son. For he would treat young Byron as his own. Two people depending on him. Two people waiting for him to return from his missions for the king. Two people to mourn his passing should he fall on the field of battle.

Malcolm's steps faltered. Holy Mary Mother of God. What was he about to do?

His breath caught and stayed in his lungs. And then he felt like he might choke. No air could flow in or out.

"Malcolm? Are ye well?" Rose's sweet voice brought him

back, the air finally pushing from his lungs—and with it a measure of his panic.

Patting her hand on his arm, he smiled—genuinely. "Better than I've been in months."

He was telling the truth. Aye, he was scared half to death at the prospect of marriage, but he was also excited for the future and the unpredictability of what Rose and her son would not only bring to his life—but what he would bring to theirs. Another adventure. A new mission.

The only downside—the king was likely to rebuke him for his actions, but Robert the Bruce would understand. Sometimes, a man had to do daring things to keep those he cared for safe.

"Father Henry," Rose said calmly. "We would be honored if ye'd be willing to marry us."

"Are ye certain?" the priest asked.

"Never more," Malcolm said, standing taller. He wanted to sweep Rose up into his arms and carry her the rest of the way to Kildrummy—for he'd just realized... He was in love with her. Wholeheartedly.

"Then let us pray," Father Henry said, moving to stand on the steps outside the kirk's front entrance.

Just as he started to speak, Kavan and the rest of their unit returned, all of them standing in a semi-circle behind Rose and Malcolm, laying witness to what they would deem a miracle.

When the sun rose, it would bring with it their new beginning.

And he prayed to God, Cathal stayed away from them until he had his new wife safely behind the thick stone walls of Kildrummy.

9

They stood in the narrow entryway of the village's small tavern that housed a sleeping room above stairs for those willing to pay a fee. Rose's hands were slick, held tightly at her waist. Malcolm's hand rested at the small of her back, and while she trembled, he was sturdy and apparently calm.

Father Henry had guided them toward the inn and roused the innkeeper, who stared at them as though they were crazy, his pudgy face reddened from lack of sleep and perhaps too many mugs of his own ale. He peered around Malcolm, taking in the sight of the armed men standing guard.

"They'll not let anyone harm your establishment," Malcolm encouraged. "We need the room only for the rest of the night, and then we'll be on our way."

"Aye." The innkeeper's gaze perused Malcolm with an assessing note, then he added, "my laird."

"Captain Montgomery will do," Malcolm said.

"Aye, captain. Right this way." The man turned, holding his candle aloft. "Will ye be requiring a meal or drink?" Tentatively, he added, "A bath?"

Rose would have loved a bath, but she was thoroughly exhausted and dawn was quick approaching. She'd have to make do with the washing she did by the river earlier that evening.

"Wife?" Malcolm asked. "Do ye require anything?"

Rose shook her head. "Nay. Nothing more than perhaps a sip of whisky."

Malcolm laughed. "I could use a dram myself."

"Whisky," the innkeeper repeated. He hurried to grab a jug and two cups. "Follow me, if ye will." He meandered the stairs, his hands full to the brim.

"The man might just fall and hurt himself," Rose whispered.

"I think he's managed a time or two afore us coming along. Now, let me carry ye." Malcolm tickled her spine.

Rose shook her head, not wanting Malcolm to risk his balance on the rickety stairs. "I'm perfectly capable of walking."

"I know ye are. But I want to carry my wife up the stairs. Come now, when my parents were feeling romantic, my father always swept mother up in his arms. Did yours not?"

Rose tapped her chin. "I dinna remember."

"Then we shall make a new memory." Malcolm bent, lifting her from beneath her knees and an arm around her back as though she weighed nothing at all.

He carried her up the wobbly stairs, walking through the only door at the top, held open by the innkeeper.

The man set the whisky and cups down on a small wooden table, then mumbled goodnight before he backed out of the door and closed it behind him. Obviously in a hurry to escape any of their further requests.

Malcolm set Rose down on her feet, his hands sliding over her arms. "Ye are beautiful, Rose. Your name is verra fitting."

She smiled, both charmed and trying not to giggle with

the untethered excitement inside her. She was *married*! To Malcolm! "Ye truly are trying for romantic."

"I'll not have my wife recall her wedding night as anything other than that."

Rose raised a mocking brow, trying not to laugh, and looked around the shabby room and sagging bed.

"What?" His tone was filled with mirth. "'Tis the most gorgeous room I've ever seen." He sauntered toward her chuckling. "I can promise ye, you'll get nothing but romantic *from me*."

She laughed softly, and stroked his cheek. "Ye're doing a fine job of it, Malcolm."

"I want to please ye." He reached up, covering her hand with his, sending a shiver racing through her limbs. "I know I can never be a replacement to the man ye loved and lost, but let me try to fill the void."

She nodded. His words made her heart soar. Never could she replace her first husband, but she could find happiness again. Love...?

Heart pounding, breath heavy, she stared into Malcolm's beautiful gray eyes. They were still as turbulent as a storm, but this time, it wasn't the fierceness of battle but of passion.

"Ye already are," she whispered, reeling at the words as they spilled from her lips. And it was true. He was filling the lonely holes that her late husband had left behind. Malcolm was making her feel things again—passion, affection, desire... dare she even go so far as to say love? Was it possible? So soon?

Aye. She might be in love with him.

Could she trust herself with such a revelation? Wasn't it too late, now that they were married, to worry over things such as feelings?

Malcolm leaned down, his arms encircling her frame and brushed his lips over hers. Even just that tiny touch sent shivers cascading all over her, pushing away the turmoil and confusion going to war inside her brain. Her chest swelled, breasts feeling heavy, nipples growing taut, and a fire burned low in her belly.

She sighed against him, skimming her fingers over his stubbled jaw, down his neck and over his shoulders. She splayed her hands over his broad, firm breadth, and leaned up on tiptoe to deepen their kiss, wrapping her arms around the back of his neck. Malcolm groaned deep in his throat, a carnal sound that spoke to somewhere hidden inside her.

This was her new husband. This man, she'd just married, could kiss her like this for the rest of her days and she'd not complain over it

Malcolm traced a line over her spine, slicking his tongue between her lips to tangle with hers. The man was an incredible kisser. Demanding and giving at the same time. She felt wrapped up inside him.

They'd come up to this room to go to bed, to sleep. And yet... She hoped...

A tumble of thoughts fell through her mind. She wanted him with a deep craving she'd not felt in so long it was nearly foreign.

"Take me to bed," she whispered against his mouth, nibbling at his lower lip.

"To sleep?" he asked, his voice husky with need.

"Nay, husband. I want ye to make love to me."

Once more she found herself being lifted, only this time, his hands had skimmed down over her bottom, lifting her so that her thighs spread around his hips. "I want to take ye to the stars."

Rose smiled against his lips. "Ye are a man of a different sort, Malcolm Montgomery."

"I mean to show ye just that." He carried her toward the bed, laying her down gently, his body coming over hers, sliding his hands over her bare ankle, and pushing her gown out of the way until he clutched at her bare thighs at the sides of his hips.

He pressed his hips against hers, bracing his weight on his arms and kissed her again. When he kissed her, it was decidedly different. Hungry, aye. Passionate, aye. But this time, it held the promise of sweet sin.

Rose didn't even know that was something she could desire in a kiss.

Malcolm's body was hard and hot above her, and even though both of them were still wearing clothes, she could feel the rigid outline of his arousal against the apex of her thighs, which only served to stir her ardor further.

Any exhaustion she might have felt upon him finding her at the kirk was gone. She'd nearly died tonight. And so had he. What would she have done without him? That thought only made her hold on tighter, tears pricking her eyes. Nay, she could not cry, not when she was in his arms, not when he was eliciting such beautiful sensations.

He kissed a path down her neck, his fingers trailing in the wake of his lips, until he came to the top of her gown. Gently, he scraped the stubble of his chin over the sensitive swells of her breasts.

"Ye smell heavenly, and your skin... 'Tis like honey."

She ached for him to touch her breasts, kiss them. She was close to begging for just that when he cupped her breast with one hand, the rough pads of his fingers caressing the tender flesh. Leaning on his elbow with the opposite arm, he stroked her hair, curling tendrils around his fingers. She felt completely enfolded, cocooned in his warmth, protection and pleasure.

Delicious tingles spread over her body, making her shiver though she was anything but cold.

Rose toyed with the ends of his dark hair, glancing down

at where he rested at her breasts, his eyes on hers. He smiled, and she smiled back, like two lovers stealing out from beneath their guardian's eyes in order to share a moment of passion. Triumphant. Honest. Curious. Excited.

Malcolm kept his eyes on hers as he flicked his tongue out to stroke over the swells of her breasts. She gasped, holding in her sucked breath while his fingers reached into her gown and dragged the fabric down until her nipple was free.

Pink and puckered, her flesh fairly screamed with decadent sensation and just when she thought it might not get any better than this, his tongue flicked out to swirl over the bud. Her eyes fluttered closed, her head falling back, fingers tangling in his hair, urging him on for more.

Malcolm didn't disappoint.

He wrapped his lips around her nipple and suckled, alternating between teasing her with licks and nips and pulls. She writhed beneath him, wanting to shred away her clothes and feel the length of his hard body on top of hers—fully nude.

Aye, she'd had him pressed naked against the length of her before in the woods, but the fabric of her gown had barred her from feeling every ridge of sinew and now, she desperately wanted to. All inhibitions gone, primal need had taken over.

Rose grappled for his shirt, tugging it free from the waist of his plaid, her hands splaying over the smooth skin of his back.

Malcolm's skin was hot. Searing.

Rose gasped, her eyes slipping closed as his lips continued their delicious torment at her breasts.

"I've never..." Malcolm's words trailed off as he leaned up, cupping the side of her face, his thumb brushing over her cheek. His gaze locked with hers, and there was an intensity to his eyes that made her shiver and filled her with excitement all at once. "Rose, I am yours. Now and forever."

Before she could respond, before she could say, aye, she was his, Malcolm's lips were once more on hers. Tender, carnal, seductive. She surrendered herself to him wholeheartedly. They grappled with each others' clothes, bits of fabric flinging this way and that. One thud and then another as his boots hit the floor. A cluster of clinks as weapons, belts and brooch were tossed.

The sultry air of the room enclosed the two of them in the warmth of their embrace.

Skin on skin at last, Rose pressed her lips to his solid shoulder, her fingers roaming over his back, his ribs, his chest. She couldn't stop touching him, exploring. Malcolm leaned back on his knees, his fingers dragging between her breasts and down to her belly. Rose couldn't help the quiver his touch elicited, or the direction her eyes roamed. His body was even more impressive in the dim light of a single candle than it was with the beam of the moon.

Broad shoulders, tight muscles. A sprinkle of dark hair brushed over his chest and trailing toward his navel—and then lower. To the place where his muscles formed a natural V and his arousal, good god...

Rose drew in a breath, words unable to form at the length and breadth of *him*. She'd not seen a man more endowed. And while she thought she should have been scared, between her thighs seemed to only twinge and grow slicker with unexpected increase in need.

"Do I please ye in the light?" he asked.

She swallowed around her swollen tongue, then croaked. "Aye, husband. Much."

"Ye are the verra image of a man's dream," he whispered.

His honeyed words made her smile, made her love him all the more. For she was certain now, more than ever, that though they'd started this journey in a far different mindset, that she'd made the right choice in agreeing to be his.

Rose reached for him, her fingers trailing up his arms, she clutched him, tugging him close. Malcolm braced himself over her, the weight of his shaft pressing against her slickened folds sending another mighty frisson of yearning somersaulting through her.

He kissed her, tangling his tongue with hers as he rocked over her and against her. Teasing, toying. Every limb trembled. Every pore screamed for more of his touch. But most of all, she wanted him to claim her. Rose lifted her hips, rubbing her pelvis against his, begging for him to enter, to drive swift and deep. And yet he toyed with her. Massaging her breasts, her buttocks, her hips. Sensation built, warm and heady in her womb, and she gasped at the profound pleasure of their bodies undulating.

Malcolm kissed his way from her mouth to the column of her throat, nibbling at her collarbone. He slid his tongue between the valley of her breasts all the way down her abdomen, swirling around her navel. Rose gasped, murmuring her delight. And then she pushed up on her elbows, staring in wonder at her husband whose mouth hovered over her nether region.

"What...?" She could barely get the word out.

Malcolm slid his palms along her inner thighs, opening her to him, his eyes hooded and dark as he gazed on her feminine core.

"I'm going to kiss ye," he said.

"Kiss me?" She licked her lips watching his grin grow wicked and full of roguish intent.

"Oh, aye, wife, and I'm going to enjoy it verra much."

Rose fell back on the straw mattress as his tongue darted out, skimming along the seam of her sex and swirling around the throbbing part that felt like sparks and flames and all things decadent and sinful.

"Oh my..." she breathed, moaning, and tucking her legs up to give him better access.

Malcolm chuckled as he licked and sucked and nibbled. Sensations whipped through her faster than her mind could work. She stopped trying to concentrate on every move his tongue made and instead relished the feel of it. The heat. The pulsing. The need.

Whimpers escaped her unbidden. Her hands fisted in his hair, tugging and pushing at the same time. The world as she knew it vanished. Making love to Byron had always been pleasurable and exciting, but this... This was something entirely different, and saints but she was enjoying it. And she was extremely glad that there was some part of making love that she could experience anew with Malcolm.

And just like that, waves of infinite pleasure shattered her. She squeezed her thighs against his face, moaning, and then jerking them back open when she realized she was probably squeezing the breath from her husband. Entire body trembling, the effects of her climax still pulsing through her, Rose let her arms fall languidly to her sides.

Malcolm skimmed his broad frame up the length of her, his abdomen and then his thick shaft sliding over the sensitive skin of her inner thighs and sex.

"I dare say ye enjoyed that," he drawled.

"Aye." She opened her eyes, peeking up at him with a satiated smile.

"But we're not done yet." He kissed her, the scent of her essence on his lips. Rather than turn away, she melted, tasting what he'd tasted. Musky, sweet.

Malcolm massaged her hips, lifting her thighs up and urging her to tuck them around his middle, and then he was probing her opening with the head of his arousal. Once more the same sparks of carnal sensation grabbed hold. She moaned, lifting her pelvis closer. He notched himself against her and thrust hard, entering her in one long, thick drive.

Both of them cried out as he buried himself to the hilt. Zounds but it was divine.

As he began to move, his body syncing with hers, she realized that pleasure had no limits. The divine became ecstasy and every thrust, every tilt of her hips, every kiss, every whispered word and soft caress, brought her to new heights of boundless pleasure.

"Och, love, ye're driving me mad," Malcolm whispered. "Ye feel so good wrapped around me."

Rose answered with a moan, her thighs clutching his hips, her fingers holding tight to his back. Ripples of muscle worked beneath her fingertips, over her, inside her. Malcolm increased his pace, thrusting deep and arcing up, pulling out, plunging hard, swiveling, she couldn't keep track, but held on for dear life as he brought her to the precipice of pleasure and flung her free.

Rose cried out, back arching, body tightening as release once more shattered inside her. Malcolm, growled, driving faster, harder, pounding against her, riding out her waves and then he too was crying out, moaning deep and guttural, utterly virile. Her skin sizzled. Thighs quivered, fingers trembled.

"Beautiful," Malcolm whispered, his forehead falling to hers. "There is no other word."

Rose cupped his face and kissed him tenderly. "Aye, there is. Bliss. Hope."

❧ 10 ❧

Malcolm settled his wife in front of him, his cock hardening as soon as she wiggled her bonny arse. Och, but after making love to her three times through the night, he was certain he'd be hard for the rest of his days. Rose was a passionate, excitable, giving lover—but even beyond that, she intrigued him much.

Though she was not a tender youth, and had been married once before, there was still so much about her that was innocent and eager. He'd not expected it, and it gave him hope that their marriage would be stimulating both mentally and physically.

"Not much longer. A day's ride and then we'll be at Kildrummy," he said.

"And I'll see my son." The excitement in her voice was palpable.

"Aye, love. Ye'll soon be reunited with the lad. I canna wait to meet him."

"He's a little hellion, but he'll like ye, Malcolm. He's been fascinated by swords and warriors since before he could walk and talk."

"If he's anything like his mother, I'm certain to enjoy his company greatly."

Rose settled against him, and he held her close, still surprised at how right it felt for her to be in his arms when for so many years he'd been set against it.

The journey was a mixture of slow trekking over the ridges, quickened by the downhill fast riding over sloping heaths. Though it sprinkled a few times, there were no torrential downpours, and even the spritzes of rain did not slow them down. Scouts reported every hour, and none had yet to see the Mackenzies following.

When mid-day arrived, the sun hidden behind faintly gray clouds, Malcolm helped his wife down from Lucifer and wrapped an extra plaid around her shivering shoulders.

"'Tis cold without the sun," she remarked.

"Aye. But I've a way to keep ye warm." He leaned down to trace his tongue suggestively over her ear.

Rose gasped and swatted at him. "Not in the daylight with all your men about."

"Och, but they dinna care."

Rose stared at his lips a moment, and then raised her chin, managing to look down her nose at him, even though he towered over her. "I willna be seen as that type of woman."

Malcolm held in his laughter, finding her sudden prudish demeanor quite humorous given how passionate she'd been the night before. "*That* type?"

She crossed her arms, either warding off his advances or keeping herself from touching him. Malcolm liked to think it was the latter.

"One who dallies."

Malcolm laughed. "I dinna think it is considered dallying when 'tis your husband ye dally with."

"What is it called then?"

Malcolm nearly choked on a laugh at what his first

response was, and then the second... He held back what he wanted to say, as the image of their bodies writhing in ecstasy came to mind. Already his plaid was starting to rise behind his sporran. So instead, he went for what he found funny—and what was guaranteed to get a rise out of her. "'Tis called a duty."

"A duty, ye say?" Her arms dropped, fingers toying the King Richard Dagger at her hip, a silent message as to what she thought of his opinion.

"Aye," he grinned, knowing he was about to pique her anger and enjoying every minute of it. "As my wife, ye ought to please me when I ask."

Her frown caused such deep grooves in her face he caught just a glimpse of what she'd look like when they were old and gray.

"Humph. I know 'tis that way for most of ye brutes, but I've been a wife before and not been asked to do such. And I dinna intend to change that." She crossed her arms over her chest to hide the way her nipples pebbled beneath her gown, but not before he'd seen them.

Malcolm slid the pads of his fingers over the curve of her cheek, rubbed his thumb over her lower lip. Then he said in a low, gruff voice, "I'd never ask ye to do anything ye didna want."

"Truly?" Still she looked skeptical.

"Aye." He leaned forward and kissed her gently. Sliding his lips over hers, there was a moment when he'd intended his kiss to be sweet, but that moment passed. He slid his tongue along the seam of her lips, probing the entrance until she opened for him, and then he claimed her. Kissed her with all the sensual intent he had built up inside him. Kissed her until she whimpered, and clutched onto him. "I want to hear ye beg for it, lass."

"Och!" Rose slapped at his chest. "Ye've been teasing me all along. Ye're an animal."

Malcolm laughed and winked. "Nay, wife, a man. A man who verra much wants to please his wife. Come now, I'll see ye settled for the nooning."

Malcolm accompanied his wife to a copse of trees where he gave her privacy to take care of her needs, forcing himself not to drag her to the ground and make sweet, passionate love to her, though that was what he truly wanted. When she was finished, he escorted her back to their horses. The men had already begun to ration out the jerky, bannocks and a few apples they'd gathered.

Malcolm laid out a plaid on the ground a little bit away from their group to give them some measure of privacy, and laid before her as best a feast he could make from their traveling provisions. They settled with their backs to the men. Rose ate with the gusto of a lad just grown into his body.

"Hungry, love?" he asked.

"Never had a bannock that tasted so sweet," she giggled. "Though I suspect I'm hungry for other reasons."

"And they would be?"

Her face pinkened, eyes went skittish. She bit one voluptuous lip and he was done. He lifted her up, settling her on his lap and licked the apple's juice from her lips.

"Now I know why my brother Jamie gave up his missions for his wife Lorna," he murmured against her mouth. "I canna imagine a day going by without ye near me."

"I'd never ask ye to give up your livelihood." Rose threaded her fingers through his hair, tugging gently until he kissed her again.

"I thank ye for that, but 'tis something I may have to consider. Else I pack ye in my satchel and take ye with me everywhere I go."

She bit his lip, teasing. "I dinna think that will be verra comfortable for me. I'm not that small."

"Small enough to fit on my lap." He gazed seductively into her eyes. "The perfect size for me to slide inside..." He trailed fingers beneath her skirt, up the inside of her calf, swirling a circle beneath her knee.

Rose gasped and tried to shove his hand away, but he wouldn't be deterred in what he sought.

"Your men," she whispered, frantically, her eyes already going darker with hunger.

"They canna see me." He tickled her inner thigh, and leaned close to her ear. "Open just a little for me. I promise ye'll like it."

Rose let out an exaggerated sigh, the intent of her mock annoyance lost in the sigh of pleasure she gave when he cupped her heat. Hell, but her sex was hot and slick. Malcolm was instantly hard as stone.

He nuzzled her cheek, kissing her chin, while he slid his fingers along the satin folds. She trembled in his lap.

"Kiss me, Rose," he said.

There was no protest as she eagerly latched her lips on his, kissing him with the passion she'd shown him the night before. Whimpers escaped her throat, her breath hitching when he slid two fingers deep inside her delicious channel. He could practically taste the honeyed sweetness of her on his tongue. Lord, if his men were not there, he'd toss up her gown and dine on her forbidden fruit once more.

"Gods, lass, I love the way ye respond to me. So wet... So hot... So seductive." He teased her nub, smiling against her lips when she shifted her hips to gain more of his touch.

He worked her with his fingers, in and out, rubbing, all while she kissed him hard, and then her body was tightening around him, shuddering. Malcolm stole her breath with his tongue, swallowing her cry of release, and nearly coming undone himself when her muscles tightened on his fingers.

Slipping from inside her. He pressed his forehead to hers. "I want to do that everyday," he said.

"I want to pleasure ye," she said. "Just as ye have done for me."

Malcolm shook his head, though his cock eagerly bobbed its head in agreement. "We canna. *That,* my men will certainly notice."

"How so? Our backs are to them."

"I've a better idea." Malcolm tugged her up to standing and led her back toward the copse of trees until they were no longer in sight of the men. "Now, no one can see us."

"Tell me what ye like," she said, her eager eyes on him.

"I want to be inside ye," he said.

A grin, mischievous and wicked curled her rose-kissed lips. When she dropped to her knees before him, her hands sliding beneath his kilt to splay on his thighs, Malcolm stiffened else he fall over.

"Wife..." Saints, but he'd forgotten Rose was no blushing virgin, but a woman once happily married before.

"Let me."

Before he could deny her, Rose's hands had found his hardened shaft, circling the base, and her head disappeared beneath his plaid. Thank the heavens for the tree behind him, because as soon as her lips brushed over the head of his cock he needed the trunk to brace himself.

"Och... Rose," he growled.

She wrapped her luscious lips around him, and slid him into the heated velvet of her mouth.

Malcolm muffled a curse and groaned. He'd died and floated all the way to accept his final reward. He lifted his plaid from her head, wanting to watch her fiery locks as she bobbed up and down along the length of him. He tenderly cupped the back of her head, threading her soft hair between his fingers. There was never a more erotic sight than his lovely wife sucking his cock.

She worked him like magic, and he was lost. There was no way to keep control, not with her tongue swirling around the thickness of him, not with her hand working in tandem with her mouth. Up, down. Wet. Hot. Soft. Hard.

Malcolm gave up the fight, his head falling back, and a guttural moan forcing its way from his throat as a release took hold with barreling power. *Fuck*! She was good...

He tugged her up, hauling her against him, using the hem of his shirt to wipe at her pink-swollen lips.

"Ye're full of surprises," he said.

A seductive smile curled her lips. "All of them good?"

He kissed her mouth. "Aye."

When they returned from the woods, they packed up their meal and returned to the horses, Rose's face flushed pink, and Malcolm unable to stop grinning. He felt like a merry fool, but he didn't give a damn. For the first time in his life, he was certain of his happiness.

They rode out, the rest of their journey filled with chatter, laughter and a long nap for Rose. By the time they crested the last of the mountains, Kildrummy's four towers loomed on the horizon.

"There, 'tis," Malcolm said, realizing his wife slept.

Rather than wake her, they rode the rest of the way to the castle, the sun having sunk by the time they arrived at the gates.

The portcullis was raised and they made their way into the bailey, but they were not greeted with a joyful reunion. The men grimaced, worry creasing their brows.

"What is it," Malcolm demanded.

"The Mackenzies got the boy," Warrec, Malcolm's trusted

guard said as he approached. "A few miles back, they ambushed us."

"When?"

"Not an hour ago."

"So they've not gotten far?"

"Nay, we came back for reinforcements."

"My son!" Rose darted out of her sleep, her head slamming against the bottom of Malcolm's chin, but even that pain would not be as sharp as what she'd just learned. "Where is he?"

Malcolm's gut wrenched. "I will get him back. I promise."

HOW COULD SHE HAVE SHARED THOSE TENDER MOMENTS with Malcolm when her son was being terrorized and abducted for the second time in the last week? Rose's heart clenched tight and painfully behind her ribs. Her eyes were wide, filled with tears that she refused to let spill. 'Twas her fault. If she'd not allowed her husband to pleasure her, not acted like a wanton fool, dropping to her knees in the woods, then they could have arrived in time to stop the Mackenzies from taking her child.

What an utter, idiotic fool she was!

She'd never let it happen again.

Never.

Even as the words crossed her mind she knew them to be wrong. They'd had to stop the horses to rest. And even if she'd arrived earlier, how could she have stopped an ambush? If Cathal truly wanted to take her son, he would have done it whether or not she was there. But the realizations didn't make her feel any better.

Malcolm fairly tossed her from the horse and into a guard's grip, and before Rose even had her footing on the ground, her husband was gone, his men following, bellows being shouted.

He could not leave without her!

Rose lifted her skirts in fisted grip and ran toward the gates. She had to go. She had to be there for her son.

But the guards blocked her way, shaking their heads.

She was a prisoner.

The wedding a sham!

"Let me pass," she demanded in her deepest, most authoritative voice.

"We canna, my lady."

"I demand ye open those gates now, or I'll—"

"Come inside, my dear."

Rose whipped around to see a woman with smoky-colored eyes and reddish-gold hair. Her features were sharp, stern, but beautiful nonetheless.

Straightening her shoulders, Rose shook her head. "Nay. I want my son. I'll get him back myself."

The woman smiled. A ginger-haired handsome warrior placed his arm around the woman's shoulder.

"I daresay ye would," the man said, nodding, his face serious. "But not even my wife, Lady Julianna, plans to accompany the men this time."

Lady Julianna... Rose searched her mind, realizing that standing before her was Robert the Bruce's half-sister, a warrior in her own right. And the man beside her must have been Ronan Sutherland. Cousin to Daniel.

"Ye must understand. My boy. He will be frightened. He *needs* me."

"Malcolm will bring him back. I'll see to it." Daniel Murray ran past her toward the stables, followed by a horde of other men.

Daniel had made it? Relief flooded her. Someone she knew, trusted.

She turned to run after him. "Daniel!" Rose shouted, but Julianna stayed her.

Rose wrenched free, ready to race after her brother-by-marriage.

"Daniel and Malcolm are verra capable, my lady. As am I." Ronan kissed Julianna and then he too was gone.

Mind spinning, heart racing like a thousand horses, Rose shivered and hugged herself. Her knees wobbled and she worried very much that she would fall. Her stomach roiled and she thought she might be ready to vomit. She gagged.

Julianna touched her shoulder. "Come inside. I will wait with you. I will pray with you."

Rose shook her head. She couldn't go inside. She just couldn't.

"Is Myra here?" Rose asked. She needed the comfort of someone familiar. Julianna was a stranger to her.

"Aye. Come inside. She was preparing your chamber, though I told her not to fuss, that the servants would do it, but she wanted ye to be comfortable."

"I will share Malcolm's chamber," Rose mumbled without thinking. It was only the gasp from Julianna that reminded her no one yet knew of their marriage.

"That would be scandalous," Julianna said. "Ye cannot."

Rose sighed, gritting her teeth. "I'm certain 'tis not. He is my husband." Rose touched the hilt of King Richard's dagger at her hip. If Malcolm didn't get her son back, she'd make certain he paid the rest of his days—nay, the hours, she'd let him live.

The inside of the castle was warm, though a draft blew a subtle breeze around Rose's ankles. But it only made her fear for her son, and to worry over whether or not he was warm or cold. Julianna led her into the great hall where several people stood or sat in conversation.

Rose immediately spotted Myra, who glanced up from who she was speaking with and looked as though she was ready to bolt toward her, but kept her cool all the same.

"Myra is speaking with Queen Elizabeth and the Bruce's brother Nigel," Julianna said.

Rose looked at the back of Robert the Bruce's new bride's head, so elegantly plaited in winding loops around her head, with a small crown atop. Beside her, the man named Nigel looked fierce and intent.

"Your Grace, if I may present Sir Malcolm's bride, Lady Rose of Munro."

Rose wanted to melt into the floor. She should not have blurted out the information to Julianna. There could have possibly been time to annul the marriage, though it had been consummated. But still... Malcolm had blinded her from her responsibilities. Her son...

If he didn't bring him back...

Grinding her teeth until her face pulsed, Rose nodded.

Myra's mouth had fallen open at the news, but Rose avoided her gaze. Her mind was not in this. She was worried about Byron. Poor lad had to be frightened out of his wits, not to mention that she was certain that Cathal Mackenzie wanted nothing more than to do away with her child. What if he'd already...

The introductions were exchanged, but Rose could barely say a word, though she did manage to curtsy to her new queen.

"Ye must be exhausted," Myra said. "Your Grace, would ye mind overmuch if I took Lady Rose to her room and saw that a bath was brought up?"

The queen smiled, kindness in her eyes. "Of course. The king will want to speak with ye soon."

"I am his loyal servant," Rose murmured, hoping the king would in fact *not* wish to see her. She'd not be able to concentrate a wit on any real conversation. All she could think of was her child, and begrudgingly, she worried over Malcolm's safety.

Myra looped her arm through Rose's and led her up a winding stair. "I am so sorry about all this," she was saying. "If we'd known about Cathal then we never would have..."

But her words were lost on Rose who barely noticed how many flights they'd climbed, or which door she'd been led down which corridor. Inside, a bath sat before a hearth, already filled with warm water and behind her, Myra was unplaiting Rose's hair and tugging off her clothes. She sank into the warmth of the tub, listening to Myra's chatter, but not at all certain what she was saying.

A glass of wine was thrust into her grip, but Rose couldn't drink. Not when her child's life was in danger.

"I need him back," she said.

Myra frowned. "I'm sorry to have jabbered on like I did when what ye needed is comfort. Daniel, Ronan and Malcolm will bring him back. The Mackenzies had only just ambushed the men an hour's ride from the castle, not too long before ye arrived. The way I saw them riding out, there's no doubt they've already come upon the blasted fools."

Rose squeezed her eyes shut and shook her head. She didn't want to think about that and what that could mean. Her child, in the middle of a vicious battle. For she'd seen what it could be when he wasn't even present.

Myra pulled Rose from the tub, dried her and helped her to dress. She brushed her hair until it dried and crackled with each stroke.

"God would not have saved your bairn once only to see him harmed by Cathal Mackenzie," Myra said, conviction in her voice. "Shall I pray with ye?"

Rose nodded. She dropped to her knees, fingers laced, murmuring frantically to her God.

An hour, or maybe two, later a loud raucous noise sounded from the courtyard. Rose and Myra's eyes locked.

"Either we're under attack, or the men have returned," Myra said.

Rose was on her feet, out the door and running before she registered Myra calling her back to go the opposite way. She rushed down the circular stair, slapping her hand against the stone to catch her balance every time she nearly fell. They burst through the main doors out into the courtyard to see a hundred warriors, easily, slapping each other on the back, blood smeared on their hands.

Not an attack.

The men had returned.

They seemed jovial.

Had to mean her son...

"Byron!" she screamed. "Byron!" Rose twisted about searching the sea of bodies, but not recognizing the tiny form of her child.

She ran through the throng, shoving grown men aside.

"Mama!" The sound of Byron's sweet voice made her heart ache.

Rose turned around to see him rushing toward her. She dropped to the ground, no longer able to stand and held out her arms as he threw himself against her. He shook in her embrace, and she realized that most of it was indeed her own trembling at nearly having lost him.

"My darling, my bairn," she sobbed against his shoulder, stroking his soft hair and hugging him tight. She breathed in his familiar, childlike scent, every memory since the day he was born fleeting through her mind. She pulled away to plant kisses all over his face. "I love ye so much."

"I love ye, too, mama." Byron beamed. "I was saved by a hero."

Rose leaned back on her heels, looking into her son's bright and excited face. She stroked his cheeks. "A hero?"

"Aye, mama. A man who looks like the devil but is an angel in disguise."

Malcolm. There was no other way to describe him.

"Out of the mouths of bairns." The deep rumbling of her husband's voice had Rose startling.

She whipped around to see Malcolm standing behind her. She wanted to hug him and slap him all at once. To keep herself from doing just that, she determined to do neither. Taking Byron's hand, she slowly stood to face her husband. Her heart lurched and again the urge to throw herself against him shot through her. She'd not realized how grateful she would be to see *him* returned to her, safe.

"Cathal Mackenzie will never bother ye again. I've made certain of it." His words spoke of the finality of death.

All the thoughts of an annulment, of hating him, murdering him even, had been just that, thoughts. Anger at the possible loss of her son. And justified, too. But it didn't matter. She still loved him. Fiercely.

A knot shaped in her throat and she couldn't make words form. But she didn't need to. Malcolm wrapped her in his embrace and hugged her tight, burying his face in her hair.

"Ye are not hurt?" she asked.

"Nothing more than a scratch. I told ye, I'd die before letting those bastards take your child. I'll protect him and ye the rest of my days."

"Ye made me a vow, Sir Malcolm, on the blade of your ruby dagger, that ye would protect me, and now it extends to my son." She leaned up, allowing Malcolm to touch his fervent lips to hers. "And thank ye."

"Oh, aye, lass," he said against her mouth. "Ye have my pledge for all the days of my life."

"Mama?" Byron's questioning voice broke into their rushed actions and Rose leapt back.

She stared down at her boy and ruffled his hair, then tugged him against her hip. "Son, I'd like ye to meet Sir Malcolm, my husband."

Byron's silence was deafening and Rose thought she might very well have to take him and run away, but then he grabbed hold of Malcolm's hand, studying his long, thick fingers.

"Ye married the devil's angel, mama?"

Rose and Malcolm both laughed. "Aye, I suppose I did. But there is nothing evil about Malcolm. He is all goodness." She stared right at Malcolm. "And I love him."

Malcolm's eyes widened and for once she thought she

might have stunned him speechless, but then he reached for her, stroked her cheek, "I love ye, too, Rose."

Clapping sounded from somewhere and Rose and Malcolm looked to see their king, Robert the Bruce, striding toward them, his wife by his side. "I see ye've completed your mission," the king said.

Malcolm nodded, straightening his shoulders. "Aye, I have delivered them to ye, Your Grace, but I'm afraid, I have some rather... urgent news."

She'd not have thought it possible, but Malcolm's fingers trembled slightly inside hers. Before he could continue, she broke in. "I forced Sir Malcolm to marry me."

The Bruce winged a brow and looked at her skeptically. "Is that so?"

"Aye."

"I find it rather curious that a lady, capable though I'm certain ye are, could force one of my fiercest warriors into anything."

"Ye'd be surprised," she said, not certain what else to say. She wasn't very good at lying. Everyone could always see right through her, and she guessed the king was no exception.

Then the king broke out into laughter. "All's well that ends well," he said. "Ye see, I was going to decree the two of ye wed when he brought ye back anyway."

"Your Grace..." Malcolm said, kneeling.

Rose and Byron, too, knelt before their king.

The king waved away whatever it was her husband was about to say. "Ye dinna need to say anything more. I know what happened with Cathal. 'Tis the reason Laird Murray and his lady wife are in attendance. My sister, God bless her, came across intelligence regarding Cathal while she was traveling north, and she relayed it to Daniel who when finding Foulis clear, came to see me straight away."

"There is something," Rose said, shifting her gaze from

the Bruce to Malcolm. "I thought my maid had hallucinated the scene, but after our betrothal contract was signed, Cathal left suddenly. Our maid swore she saw him riding off with an English garrison. But she was also unreliable..." She rubbed her temples. "I'm so sorry. If I had believed her..."

"Dinna worry over it, lass. Ye are not at fault here. The man was corrupt and now we no longer have to worry over him." The Bruce held out his hand, squeezing hers gently.

"I must offer my heartiest apologies for marrying without your permission," Malcolm said. "Even if ye would have ordered it upon our return. I—"

"Enough," the Bruce interrupted. "There is no further need for explanation. 'Twas high time ye married and I'm glad 'twas a choice ye made on your own. Makes for a happier marriage. Though sometimes we do get lucky." He winked at his wife. "Now, in other great rewards, I must also confer upon ye your new title."

Malcolm bowed his head and Rose beamed with pride. She'd need a week to recover from all this excitement happening in so short a time.

"I dub thee, Sir Malcolm Montgomery, Guardian of the North Sea, and in partnership with Lady Rose Munro, guardians of Laird Byron Munro and Chief Regents of Clan Munro, until the lad comes of age. Rise."

Malcolm rose, tugging Rose and her child up, too. "Ye have my endless gratitude and always my service," he said to the king.

"And ye have mine," Robert the Bruce answered. "Now, let us feast!"

Whatever exhaustion Rose had felt before was now fully gone. All she wanted to do was dance and cheer and hug her loved ones close.

Their lives could have turned out so much different than they had. She couldn't help but send a prayer of thanks up to the heavens, for there had to have been some bit of divine intervention in all that had occurred.

Holding tight to her husband with one hand and her son with the other, Rose followed the crowd of revelers into Kildrummy Castle.

EPILOGUE

4 months later, mid-August
Foulis Castle

"The king has been defeated at Lorne, and I've left his wife in the care of his brother Nigel at Kildrummy."

Rose rubbed her husband's taut shoulders with soap, bunched with the stress of the ride, their latest battle, the state of the Scots' will to forge ahead even without William Wallace at their lead. His death had not done what the English wished—to squash the Scots' desire for independence. Quite the opposite.

She'd had a bath drawn immediately upon Malcolm's return and ordered him into the tub without delay, hoping to ease some of his worry.

"What will he do?" she asked softly, stroking a wet cloth over his skin.

Malcolm shook his head, leaning back, his head resting on her thighs, covered by only her chemise and his hand coming to rest on hers where she washed him. "I dinna know. 'Tis as though we take one step forward, only to take another back. Our men are defeated, they are tired."

"They still have heart for their country."

"They do. I do."

"Then they will never stop until they are free."

"Aye."

The little flutter bounced around inside her womb. The one she'd been waiting over a month to tell him about since he'd been gone.

He leaned back further, his eyes locking on hers. "For now, all I wish to do is lay in my wife's arms until dawn."

Rose kissed his washed hair. "Then let it be so. There will be more than enough time to plan and talk battle later. For now, let us celebrate that ye are home safe and sound. And I've another bit of news, too."

"Is all well with Byron?" he asked, glancing up at her.

"Aye, he is well."

"And the villagers? The crops?"

Rose smiled. "They all flourish."

"The port?" he groaned.

Rose suppressed a giggle. "Safe."

"What then? Tell me."

Rose traced the lines away from his brow. "I am to have your bairn."

"What?" Malcolm bolted upright in the tub and turned as much as he could with his sizable bulk to stare at her. "A bairn? My bairn?"

Rose laughed. "Aye, husband. *Your* bairn. A child we two created grows within my womb."

"Saints, lassie, that is the verra best news." Somehow, he twisted enough to tug her, chemise and all, into his lap.

Rose yelped as the water sloshed, soaking her chemise.

Thank goodness she'd taken her gown off so as not to get it wet while she washed him.

"Byron will make a good older brother," Malcolm mused.

"Aye, and ye'll make a good father."

Her husband grinned, his white teeth flashing and his smoky eyes taking her all in as his hand stroked over her slightly rounded belly. "Thank ye, Rose, for showing me what I was missing in my life."

"Nay, thank ye, husband, for abducting me." Rose couldn't help the teasing slant to her smile.

Malcolm shook his head, an answering grin on his face. "Bah, ye'll never allow me to live that down will ye, now?"

"Not ever."

"Then, 'haps I can make ye forget it for a moment." He nuzzled her neck, then captured her lips in a searing kiss, while his fingers toyed with her puckered nipples.

Zounds, but she'd missed this.

Malcolm stood, lifting her into his arms, and soaking wet, carried her through their sultry room to their bed, where the ruby dagger shined against the stone wall where it was mounted above the headboard. He tossed her, wet chemise and all.

"Och, ye'll ruin the sheets! They're soaked!" she shrieked, though not at all bothered as he came down hard atop her.

"Soaked with water, soaked with sweat, we'll ruin these sheets together."

And no other words were needed, for in truth, she very much looked forward to the ruining.

If you enjoyed **TAKEN BY THE HIGHLANDER***, please spread the word by leaving a review on the site where you purchased your copy, or a reader site such as Goodreads or Shelfari! I love to hear from readers too, so drop me a line at* authoreliza-knight@gmail.com *OR visit me on Facebook:*

https://www.facebook.com/elizaknightauthor. I'm also on Twitter: @ElizaKnight. If you'd like to receive my occasional newsletter, please sign up at www.elizaknight.com. *Many thanks!*

EXCERPT FROM THE HIGHLANDER'S GIFT

An injured Warrior...

Betrothed to a princess until she declares his battle wound has incapacitated him as a man, Sir Niall Oliphant is glad to step aside and let the spoiled royal marry his brother. He's more than content to fade into the background with his injuries and remain a bachelor forever, until he meets the Earl of Sutherland's daughter, a lass more beautiful than any other, a lass who makes him want to stand up and fight again.

A lady who won't let him fail...

As daughter of one of the most powerful earls and Highland chieftains in Scotland, Bella Sutherland can marry anyone she wants—but she doesn't want a husband. When she spies an injured warrior at the Yule festival who has been shunned by the Bruce's own daughter, she decides a husband in name only might be her best solution.

They both think they're agreeing to a marriage of convenience, but love and fate has other plans...

CHAPTER ONE

Dupplin Castle
Scottish Highlands
Winter, 1318

Sir Niall Oliphant had lost something.

Not a trinket, or a boot. Not a pair of hose, or even his favorite mug. Nothing as trivial as that. In fact, he wished it *was* so minuscule that he could simply replace it. What'd he'd lost was devastating, and yet it felt entirely selfish given some of those closest to him had lost their lives.

He was still here, living and breathing. He was still walking around on his own two feet. Still handsome in the face. Still able to speak coherently, even if he didn't want to.

But he couldn't replace what he'd lost.

What he'd lost would irrevocably change his life, his entire future. It made him want to back into the darkest corner and let his life slip away, to forget about even having a future at all. To give everything he owned to his brother and say goodbye. He was useless now. Unworthy.

Niall cleared the cobwebs that had settled in his throat by slinging back another dram of whisky. The shutters in his darkened bedchamber were closed tight, the fire long ago grown cold. He didn't allow candles in the room, nor visitors. So when a knock sounded at his door, he ignored it, preferring to chug his spirits from the bottle rather than pouring it into a cup.

The knocking grew louder, more insistent.

"Go away," he bellowed, slamming the whisky down on the side table beside where he sat, and hearing the clay jug shatter. A shard slid into his finger, stinging as the liquor splashed over it. But he didn't care.

This pain, pain in his only index finger, he wanted to have. Wanted a reminder there was still some part of him left. Part of him that could still feel and bleed. He tried to ignore that part of him that wanted to be alive, however small it was.

The handle on the door rattled, but Niall had barred it the day before. Refusing anything but whisky. Maybe he could drink himself into an oblivion he'd never wake from. Then all of his worries would be gone forever.

"Niall, open the bloody door."

The sound of his brother's voice through the cracks had Niall's gaze widening slightly. Walter was a year younger than he was. And still whole. Walter had tried to understand Niall's struggle, but what man could who'd not been through it himself?

"I said go away, ye bloody whoreson." His words slurred, and he went to tipple more of the liquor only to recall he'd just shattered it everywhere.

Hell and damnation. The only way to get another bottle would be to open the door.

"I'll pretend I didna hear ye just call our dear mother a whore. Open the damned door, or I'll take an axe to it."

Like hell he would. Walter was the least aggressive one in their family. Sweet as a lad, he'd grown into a strong warrior, but he was also known as the heart of the Oliphant clan. The idea of him chopping down a door was actually funny. Outside, the corridor grew silent, and Niall leaned his head back against the chair, wondering how long he had until his brother returned, and if it was enough time to sneak down to the cellar and get another jug of whisky.

Needless to say, when a steady thwacking sounded at the door—reminding Niall quite a bit like the heavy side of an axe—he sat up straighter and watched in drunken fascination as the door started to splinter. Shards of wood came flying through the air as the hole grew larger and the sound of the axe beating against the surface intensified.

Walter had grown some bloody ballocks.

Incredible.

Didn't matter. What would Walter accomplish by breaking down the door? What could he hope would happen?

Niall wasn't going to leave the room or accept food.

Niall wasn't going to move on with his life.

So he sat back and waited, curious more than anything as to what Walter's plan would be once he'd gained entry.

Just as tall and broad of shoulder as Niall, Walter kicked through the remainder of the door and ducked through the ragged hole.

"That's enough." Walter looked down at Niall, his face fierce, reminding him very much of their father when they were lads.

"That's enough?" Niall asked, trying to keep his eyes wide but having a hard time. The light from the corridor gave his brother a darkened, shadowy look.

"Ye've sat in this bloody hell hole for the past three days."

Walter gestured around the room. "Ye stink of shite. Like a bloody pig has laid waste to your chamber."

"Are ye calling me a shite pig?" Niall thought about standing up, calling his brother out, but that seemed like too much effort.

"Mayhap I am. Will it make ye stand up any faster?"

Niall pursed his lips, giving the impression of actually considering it. "Nay."

"That's what I thought. But I dinna care. Get up."

Niall shook his head slowly. "I'd rather not."

"I'm not asking."

My, my. Walter's ballocks were easily ten times than Niall had expected. The man was bloody testing him to be sure.

"Last time I checked, I was the eldest," Niall said.

"Ye might have been born first, but ye lost your mind some time ago, which makes me the better fit for making decisions."

Niall hiccupped. "And what decisions would ye be making, wee brother?"

"Getting your arse up. Getting ye cleaned up. Airing out the gongheap."

"Doesna smell so bad in here." Niall gave an exaggerated sniff, refusing to admit that Walter was indeed correct. It smelled horrendous.

"I'm gagging, brother. I might die if I have to stay much longer."

"Then by all means, pull up a chair."

"Ye're an arse."

"No more so than ye."

"Not true."

Niall sighed heavily. "What do ye want? Why would ye make me leave? I've nothing to live for anymore."

"Ye've eight-thousand reasons to live, ye blind goat."

"Eight thousand?"

"A random number." Walter waved his hand and kicked at something on the floor. "Ye've the people of your clan, the warriors ye lead, your family. The woman ye're betrothed to marry. Everyone is counting on ye, and ye must come out of here and attend to your duties. Ye've mourned long enough."

"How can ye presume to tell me that I've mourned long enough? Ye know nothing." A slow boiling rage started in Niall's chest. All these men telling him how to feel. All these men thinking they knew better. A bunch of bloody ballocks!

"Aye, I've not lost what ye have, brother. Ye're right. I dinna know what 'tis like to be ye, either. But I know what 'tis like to be the one down in the hall waiting for ye to come and take care of your business. I know what 'tis like to look upon the faces of the clan as they worry about whether they'll be raided or ravaged while their leader sulks in a vat of whisky and does nothing to care for them."

Niall gritted his teeth. No one understood. And he didn't need the reminder of his constant failings.

"Then take care of it," Niall growled, jerking forward fast enough that his vision doubled. "Ye've always wanted to be first. Ye've always wanted what was mine. Go and have it. Have it all."

Walter took a step back as though Niall had hit him. "How can ye say that?" Even in the dim light, Niall could see the pain etched on his brother's features. Aye, what he'd said was a lie, but it had made him feel better all the same.

"Ye heard me. Get the fuck out." Niall moved to push himself from the chair, remembered too late how difficult that would be, and fell back into it. Instead, he let out a string of curses that had Walter shaking his head.

"Ye need to get yourself together, decide whether or not ye are going to turn your back on this clan. Do it for yourself. Dinna go down like this. Ye are still Sir Niall fucking

Oliphant. Warrior. Heir to the chiefdom of Oliphant. Hero. Leader. Brother. Soon to be husband and father."

Walter held his gaze unwaveringly. A torrent of emotion jabbed from that dark look into Niall's chest, crushing his heart.

"Get out," he said again through gritted teeth, feeling the pain of rejecting his brother acutely.

They'd always been so close. And even though he was pushing him away, he also desperately wanted to pull him closer.

He wanted to hug him tightly, to tell him not to worry, that soon enough he'd come out of the dark and be the man Walter once knew. But those were all lies, for he would never be the same again, and he couldn't see how he would ever be able to exit this room and attempt a normal life.

"Ye're not the only one who's lost a part of himself," Walter muttered as he ducked beneath the door. "I want my brother back."

"Your brother is dead."

At that, Walter paused. He turned back around, a snarl poised on his lips, and Niall waited longingly for whatever insult would come out. Any chance to engage in a fight, but then Walter's face softened. "Maybe he is."

With those soft words uttered, he disappeared, leaving behind the gaping hole and the shattered wood on the floor, a haunting mirror image to the wide-open wound Niall felt in his soul.

Niall glanced down to his left, at the sleeve that hung empty at his side, a taunting reminder of his failure in battle. Warrior. Ballocks! Not even close.

When he considered lying down on the ground and licking the whisky from the floor, he knew it was probably time to leave his chamber. But he was no good to anyone outside of his room. Perhaps he could prove that fact once and for all, then Walter would leave him be. And he knew his brother spoke the truth about smelling like a pig. He'd not bathed in days. If he was going to prove he was worthless as a leader now, he would do so smelling decent, so people took him seriously rather than believing him to be mad.

Slipping through the hole in the door, he walked noiselessly down the corridor to the stairs at the rear used by the servants, tripping only once along the way. He attempted to steal down the winding steps, a feat that nearly had him breaking his neck. In fact, he took the last dozen steps on his arse. Once he reached the entrance to the side of the bailey, he lifted the bar and shoved the door open, the cool wind a welcome blast against his heated skin. With the sun set, no one saw him creep outside and slink along the stone as he made his way to the stables and the massive water trough kept for the horses. He might as well bathe there, like the animal he was.

Trough in sight, he staggered forward and tumbled head-first into the icy water.

Niall woke sometime later, still in the water, but turned over at least. He didn't know whether to be grateful he'd not drowned. His clothes were soaked, and his legs hung out on either side of the wooden trough. It was still dark, so at least he'd not slept through the night in the chilled water.

He leaned his head back, body covered in wrinkled gooseflesh and teeth chattering, and stared up at the sky. Stars dotted the inky-black landscape and swaths of clouds streaked across the moon, as if one of the gods had swiped his hand through it, trying to wipe it away. But the moon was steadfast. Silver and bright and ever present. Returning as it should each night, though hiding its beauty day after day until it was just a sliver that made one wonder if it would return.

What was he doing out here? Not just in the tub freezing

his idiot arse off, but here in this world? Why hadn't he been taken? Why had only part of him been stolen? Cut away...

Niall shuddered, more from the memory of that moment when his enemy's sword had cut through his armor, skin, muscle and bone. The crunching sound. The incredible pain.

He squeezed his eyes shut, forcing the memories away.

This is how he'd been for the better part of four months. Stumbling drunk and angry about the castle when he wasn't holed up in his chamber. Yelling at his brother, glowering at his father and mother, snapping at anyone who happened to cross his path. He'd become everything he hated.

There had been times he'd thought about ending it all. He always came back to the simple question that was with him now as he stared up at the large face of the moon.

"Why am I still here?" he murmured.

"Likely because ye havena pulled your arse out of the bloody trough."

Walter.

Niall's gaze slid to the side to see his brother standing there, arms crossed over his chest. "Are ye my bloody shadow? Come to tell me all my sins?"

"When will ye see I'm not the enemy? I want to help."

Niall stared back up at the moon, silently asking what he should do, begging for a sign.

Walter tugged at his arm. "Come on. Get out of the trough. Ye're not a pig as much as ye've been acting the part. Let us get ye some food."

Niall looked over at his little brother, perhaps seeing him for the first time. His throat felt tight, closing in on itself as a well of emotion overflowed from somewhere deep in his gut.

"Why do ye keep trying to help me? All I've done is berate ye for it."

"Aye. That's true, but I know ye speak from pain. Not from your heart."

"I dinna think I have a heart left."

Walter rolled his eyes and gave a swift tug, pulling him halfway from the trough. Though Niall was weak from lack of food and too much whisky, he managed to get himself the rest of the way out. He stood in the moonlight, dripping water around the near frozen ground.

"Ye have a heart. Ye have a soul. One arm. That is all ye've lost. Ye still have your manhood, aye?"

Niall shrugged. Aye, he still had his bloody cock, but what woman wanted a decrepit man heaving overtop of her with his mangled body in full view.

"I know what ye're thinking," Walter said. "And the answer is, every eligible maiden and all her friends. Not to mention the kitchen wenches, the widows in the glen, and their sisters."

"Ballocks," Niall muttered.

"Ye're still handsome. Ye're still heir to a powerful clan. Wake up, man. This is not ye. Ye canna let the loss of your arm be the destruction of your whole life. Ye're not the first man to ever be maimed in battle. Dinna be a martyr."

"Says the man with two arms."

"Ye want me to cut it off? I'll bloody do it." Walter turned in a frantic circle as if looking for the closest thing with a sharp edge.

Niall narrowed his eyes, silent, watching, waiting. When had his wee brother become such an intense force? Walter marched toward the barn, hand on the door, yanked it wide as if to continue the blockhead search. Niall couldn't help following after his brother who marched forward with purpose, disappearing inside the barn.

A flutter of worry dinged in Niall's stomach. Walter wouldn't truly go through with something so stupid, would he?

When he didn't immediately reappear, Niall's pang of

worry heightened into dread. Dammit, he just might. With all the changes Walter had made recently, there was every possibility that he'd gone mad. Well, Niall might wish to disappear, but not before he made certain his brother was all right.

With a groan, Niall lurched forward, grabbed the door and yanked it open. The stables were dark and smelled of horses, leather and hay. He could hear a few horses nickering, and the soft snores of the stable hands up on the loft fast asleep.

"Walter," he hissed. "Enough. No more games."

Still, there was silence.

He stepped farther into the barn, and the door closed behind him, blocking out all the light save for a few strips that sank between cracks in the roof.

His feet shuffled silently on the dirt floor. Where the bloody hell had his brother gone?

And why was his heart pounding so fiercely? He trudged toward the first set of stables, touching the wood of the gates. A horse nudged his hand with its soft muzzle, blowing out a soft breath that tickled his palm, and Niall's heart squeezed.

"Prince," he whispered, leaning his forehead down until he felt it connect with the warm, solidness of his warhorse. Prince nickered and blew out another breath.

Niall had not ridden in months. If not for his horse, he might be dead. But rather than be irritated Prince had done his job, he felt nothing but pride that the horse he'd trained from a colt into a mammoth had done his duty.

After Niall's arm had been severed and he was left for dead, Prince had nudged him awake, bent low and nipped at Niall's legs until he'd managed to crawl and heave himself belly first over the saddle. Prince had taken him home like that, a bleeding sack of grain.

Having thought him dead, the clan had been shocked and surprised to see him return, and that's when the true battle for his life had begun. He'd lost so much blood, succumbed to fever, and stopped breathing more than once. Hell, it was a miracle he was still alive.

Which begged the question—*why, why, why*...

"He's missed ye." Walter was beside him, and Niall jerked toward his brother, seeing his outline in the dark.

"Is that why ye brought me in here?"

"Did ye really think I'd cut off my arm?" Walter chuckled. "Ye know I like to fondle a wench and drink at the same time."

Niall snickered. "Ye're an arse."

"Aye, 'haps I am."

They were silent for a few minutes, Niall deep in thought as he stroked Prince's soft muzzle. His mind was a torment of unanswered questions. "Walter, I...I dinna know what to do."

"Take it one day at a time, brother. But do take it. No more being locked in your chamber."

Niall nodded even though his brother couldn't see him. A phantom twinge of pain rippled through the arm that was no longer there, and he stopped himself from moving to rub the spot, not wanting to humiliate himself in front of his brother. When would those pains go away? When would his body realize his arm had long since become bone in the earth?

One day at a time. That was something he might be able to do. "I'll have bad days."

"Aye. And good ones, too."

Niall nodded. He longed to saddle Prince and go for a ride but realized he wasn't even certain how to mount with only one arm to grab hold of the saddle. "I have so much to learn."

"Aye. But as I recall, ye're a fast learner."

"I'll start training again tomorrow."

"Good."

"But I willna be laird. Walter, the right to rule is yours now."

"Ye've time before ye need to make that choice. Da is yet breathing and making a ruckus."

"Aye. But I want ye to know what's coming. No matter what, I canna do that. I have to learn to pull on my bloody shirt first."

Walter slapped him on the back and squeezed his shoulder. "The lairdship is yours, with or without a shirt. Only thing I want is my brother back."

Niall drew in a long, mournful breath. "I'm not sure he's coming back. Ye'll have to learn to deal with me, the new me."

"New ye, old ye, still *ye*."

Want to read the rest of ***The Highlander's Gift***?

KNIGHT

HISTORY INKED
IN DRAMA

ABOUT THE AUTHOR

Eliza Knight is an award-winning and *USA Today* bestselling author of over fifty sizzling historical romance and erotic romance. Under the name E. Knight, she pens rip-your-heart-out historical fiction. While not reading, writing or researching for her latest book, she chases after her three children. In her spare time (if there is such a thing...) she likes daydreaming, wine-tasting, traveling, hiking, staring at the stars, watching movies, shopping and visiting with family and friends. She lives atop a small mountain with her own knight in shining armor, three princesses and two very naughty puppies. Visit Eliza at http://www.elizaknight.comor her historical blog History Undressed: www.historyun-dressed.com. Sign up for her newsletter to get news about books, events, contests and sneak peaks! http://eepurl.com/CSFFD

MORE BOOKS BY ELIZA KNIGHT

THE SUTHERLAND LEGACY

The Highlander's Gift
The Highlander's Quest — *in the Ladies of the Stone anthology*
The Highlander's Stolen Bride

PIRATES OF BRITANNIA: DEVILS OF THE DEEP

Savage of the Sea
The Sea Devil
A Pirate's Bounty

THE STOLEN BRIDE SERIES

The Highlander's Temptation
The Highlander's Reward
The Highlander's Conquest

The Highlander's Lady
The Highlander's Warrior Bride
The Highlander's Triumph
The Highlander's Sin
Wild Highland Mistletoe (a Stolen Bride winter novella)
The Highlander's Charm (a Stolen Bride novella)
A Kilted Christmas Wish – a contemporary Holiday spin-off

THE CONQUERED BRIDE SERIES

Conquered by the Highlander
Seduced by the Laird
Taken by the Highlander (a Conquered bride novella)
Claimed by the Warrior
Stolen by the Laird
Protected by the Laird (a Conquered bride novella)
Guarded by the Warrior

THE MACDOUGALL LEGACY SERIES

Laird of Shadows
Laird of Twilight
Laird of Darkness

THE THISTLES AND ROSES SERIES

Promise of a Knight
Eternally Bound
Breath from the Sea

THE HIGHLAND BOUND SERIES (EROTIC TIME-TRAVEL)

Behind the Plaid
Bared to the Laird
Dark Side of the Laird
Highlander's Touch
Highlander Undone
Highlander Unraveled

WICKED WOMEN

Her Desperate Gamble
Seducing the Sheriff
Kiss Me, Cowboy

UNDER THE NAME E. KNIGHT

TALES FROM THE TUDOR COURT

My Lady Viper
Prisoner of the Queen

ANCIENT HISTORICAL FICTION

A Day of Fire: a novel of Pompeii
A Year of Ravens: a novel of Boudica's Rebellion

Made in the USA
Coppell, TX
10 May 2021

55359225R00090